Penguin Books
Death at the Chase

D0485811

Michael Innes is the pseudonym of J. I. M. Stewart who was a student of Christ Church, Oxford, from 1949 until his retirement in 1973. He was born in 1906 and was educated at Edinburgh Academy and Oriel College, Oxford. He was lecturer in English at the University of Leeds from 1930 to 1935, Jury Professor of English at the University of Adelaide, South Australia, from 1935 to 1945, and lecturer in Queen's University, Belfast, between 1946 and 1948.

He has published many novels – including the quintet *A Staircase in Surrey* (*The Gaudy, Young Pattullo, A Memorial Service, The Madonna of the Astrolabe* and *Full Term*) – several volumes of short stories, as well as books of criticism and essays, under his own name. His *Eight Modern Writers* appeared in 1963 as the final volume of *The Oxford History of English Literature*, and he is also the author of *Rudyard Kipling* (1966) and *Joseph Conrad* (1968). His most recent books are *Andrew and Tobias* (1981), *The Bridge at Arta and Other Stories* (1981) and *A Villa in France* (1982).

Under the pseudonym of Michael Innes he has written broadcast scripts and many crime novels including *Appleby's End* (1945), *The Bloody Wood* (1966), *An Awkward Lie* (1971), *The Open House* (1972), *Appleby's Answer* (1973), *Appleby's Other Story* (1974), *The Appleby File* (1975), *The Gay Phoenix* (1976), *Honeybath's Haven* (1977), *The Ampersand Papers* (1978), *Going It Alone* (1980), *Lord Mullion's Secret* (1981), *Sheiks and Adders* (1982) and *Appleby and Honeybath* (1983). Several of these are published in Penguin together with two omnibus editions, *The Michael Innes Omnibus* containing *Death at the President's Lodging, Hamlet, Revenge!* and *The Daffodil Affair* and *The Second Michael Innes Omnibus* containing *The Journeying Boy, Operation Pax* and *The Man from the Sea*.

Michael Innes

Death at the Chase

Penguin Books

Penguin Books Ltd, Harmondsworth, Middlesex, England
Viking Penguin Inc., 40 West 23rd Street, New York, New York 10010, U.S.A.
Penguin Books Australia Ltd, Ringwood, Victoria, Australia
Penguin Books Canada Limited, 2801 John Street, Markham, Ontario, Canada L3R 1B4
Penguin Books (N.Z.) Ltd, 182–190 Wairau Road, Auckland 10, New Zealand

First published in Great Britain by Victor Gollancz 1970
First published in the United States of America by Dodd, Mead & Company 1978
Published in Penguin Books 1971
Reprinted 1973, 1974, 1986

Copyright © J. I. M. Stewart, 1970
All rights reserved

The brief quotation on page 47 is from *Jealousy*
by Alain Robbe-Grillet, translated from the
French by Richard Howard, and published
in England by Calder & Boyars Ltd

Made and printed in Great Britain by
Richard Clay (The Chaucer Press) Ltd, Bungay, Suffolk
Typeset in Linotype Baskerville

Except in the United States of America, this book is sold subject
to the condition that it shall not, by way of trade or otherwise, be lent,
re-sold, hired out, or otherwise circulated without the
publisher's prior consent in any form of binding or cover other than
that in which it is published and without a similar condition
including this condition being imposed on the subsequent purchaser

Part One

A Near Thing at Ashmore Chase

1

When out walking by himself, Appleby commonly obeyed his wife Judith's rules. These – perhaps picked up from her American connections – could be summarized in the injunction, 'Go on till you're stopped'. When, on the other hand, he was accompanied by Judith, he still, after more than thirty years of companionable pedestrianism, made intermittent attempts to check her more obviously unlawful and even hazardous courses.

That a stile had not necessarily been constructed for her use, nor a fence been allowed to fall into disrepair for her convenience, were propositions which Lady Appleby was indisposed to entertain, nor could she be brought to believe that the presence of a readily negotiable hunting-gate did not of itself guarantee the absence of an un-negotiable bull. Appleby for his part, although not much given to taurophobia, had no fancy for enforced tauro-machy either, and he moreover owned a pronounced dislike of engaging uncivil landowners and surly farmers in fruitless disputation over field paths and rights of way.

But the paradox remained, and was operative with Appleby in his unaccompanied condition now. For here was this rather high wall – beginning to crumble in places, but formidable nevertheless – and inset in it a zigzag of protruding stones which made scaling it easy enough. These no doubt attracted Appleby as forming a stile more in the manner of his own north country than of this southern England where he had spent most of his working life. Perhaps because of this, or perhaps simply because it promised access to a line of higher ground from which he could hope to orient himself on his map,

Appleby hoisted himself briskly to the top of the wall. It was very improper; the stile clearly existed for somebody's shepherd or keeper, and not in the least for a retired policeman, however respectably circumstanced in the county; but Appleby was, if anything, now rather pleased with the impropriety of his proceeding. He was also pleased with the sense that his weight was right, and that his muscles were therefore more than adequate to this small athletic occasion. He celebrated this sense of well-being by not bothering to feel for the steps on the other side of the wall. He simply jumped. So he was in mid-air – a vulnerable posture – when the howl of rage assailed him.

Or had it merely been a cry of alarm? Appleby wasn't sure. But he found he had taken the precaution – by a kind of second nature, acquired in more adventurous days – of landing with his back reassuringly against the high wall he had just tumbled over. This was of course absurd. And the appearance he now saw before him, although oddly ambiguous, stopped short of being in any degree alarming. It was not for example an infuriated bull. It was only an infuriated old gentleman. But *was* he infuriated? Or was the visible trembling of his stooped and scraggy frame occasioned by some violent and sense-less alarm? It was in this that the point of ambiguity lay. The old gentleman's first utterance would no doubt re-solve the problem.

'What the devil do you mean,' the old gentleman de-manded, 'by pitching yourself into my property like that?' He took a wary step backward as he spoke, and at the same time raised in air a blackthorn walking-stick of club-like proportions. It certainly wasn't a gesture inter-pretable in terms of amiable salutation. The old gentle-man was frightened and angry together. These after all were emotions which companioned each other often enough. Only it was hard to find in the present situation much occasion for either of them.

'I am very sorry,' Appleby said pacifically. 'I must

apologize for trespassing on your land. It was simply that, noticing the stile, I thought I might venture up to the brow of the hill there, and get myself straight on the map.'

'A pretty story!' The old gentleman produced an unexpected and displeasing cackle of dry laughter. 'A very pretty story, indeed. Do you think I don't know the date?'

This irrational response to a speech which had been eminently correct naturally occasioned some indignation as well as bewilderment in Appleby. And this was rather less than assuaged when he suddenly thought he had a glimpse of what occasioned it. The old gentleman's laughter had been echoed near by by a not dissimilar sound: the harsh clattering call of a cock pheasant. This was answered by a second bird on a note of sharper challenge or alarm, and a moment later both were airborne and their dialogue fading amid a whirr of wings. The owner of these creatures – in whose presence Appleby presumably stood – was supposing himself to have apprehended a poacher. There was indeed something in his glance that supported this bizarre suspicion. He could be sensed as, so to speak, peering into Appleby's pockets as he stood – or at least as endeavouring to assess the bulk and weight of anything they might contain. That was it. This outrageous landed proprietor was supposing them filled with lengths of fishing-line, bread-pellets, and small bottles of gin.

Appleby wondered how to proceed. One possibility was to produce a visiting-card. But there was a flavour of pomposity about that; it was the sort of thing his children made fun of. Perhaps it would be better to give the equivalent information – or some of it – verbally.

'My name is Appleby,' Appleby said. 'I live about twelve miles from here, at a place called Long Dream.'

'Long Dream Manor?'

'Yes.'

'Stuff and nonsense. You're an impudent impostor.

Everard Raven lives at Dream. Old friend of mine. I see him regularly.'

Appleby opened his mouth, checked himself, and spoke gently.

'Everard Raven died about fifteen years ago. One and another thing has happened since then, and now my wife has inherited the place. We've lived there since I retired a couple of years ago.'

'Retired?' The old gentleman glowered suspiciously at Appleby as he went off at a tangent. 'Why should you have retired? You're a perfectly able-bodied man, so far as I can see. Idleness and mischief, eh?'

'I was a policeman. It's thought quite a good thing that they shouldn't hang on too long.'

'I don't believe a word of it. The Raven girls were always a queer lot, but I don't see one of them marrying a copper. Where was your last beat?'

'It wasn't exactly a beat. I was Commissioner of Metropolitan Police. Of course I was other things earlier on. And now, my dear sir, with renewed apologies, I'll take myself off your land.'

'You'll do nothing of the sort!' The old gentleman was still studying Appleby's pockets. And suddenly Appleby was visited by the fantastic notion that it wasn't a mere poacher's kit, but rather some lethal weapon, that he was suspected of carrying. Moreover the old gentleman was also *listening* – listening for something that didn't exist: footfalls, whispers, stealthy stirrings behind a bush or on the other side of the wall. The old gentleman lived in fact in some unfortunate condition of chronic anxiety. It was this perception that governed Appleby's conduct in the succeeding moments. 'You'll do nothing of the sort!' the old gentleman was repeating. 'You'll come with me to the house. This is the sort of thing that must be checked up on.' He brandished his walking-stick in a feeble but spectacular fashion. 'In front of me, please. You see the path. Quick march! *Allez-vous en, vite!*'

It was clear that neither law nor courtesy required

Appleby (who surely couldn't be taken for a Frenchman) to pay any heed to this extraordinary command. He had only to inquire whether this unreasonable person would prefer him to retreat as he had come or to terminate his trespass by some other route. It was no doubt a mixture of curiosity and compassion which prompted him to do as he had been told. He was to reflect afterwards that the mixture was an unholy one, and that he had no business to complain that trouble followed.

The house lay in a hollow, and this was no doubt the reason why Appleby hadn't spotted it earlier. It was ancient – as ancient as Dream and a good deal larger. Architecturally it would have to be called a mess, for from some nucleus which had long since been swallowed up and vanished it wandered indecisively here and there in half-timber work, red brick, and stone – and this now on one scale of pretension and now on quite another, no doubt according to the several whims and material circumstances of numerous generations of its owners. All appeared to have been very fond of chimneys; clusters of these, some weathered smooth and others still distinguishably carved with Tudor elaboration, sprouted from a grey stone roof which had turned sinuous and undulant with the years. The effect was rather that of some improbable monster in a medieval Bestiary, horripilant like the porpentine against its foes. Although the autumn day was chilly, and although the mansion scarcely had the appearance of one in which an unobtrusive central heating had been laid on, Appleby observed that from one of these numerous stacks did there come the faintest trail of smoke.

The place might have been untenanted. He began to wonder indeed if it *was* untenanted; if he was being led – or rather driven or shepherded – into some fiendish trap prepared for casual passers-by by a maniac. Perhaps when they reached the shelter of the building the old gentleman – already so unnervingly padding along behind him

– would expertly cosh him on the head with the black-thorn and then manacle him for life amid a congeries of random victims in an abandoned wine-cellar. This morbid persuasion became momentarily so strong in Appleby that he halted, turned round, and casually felt in a pocket for his pipe and tobacco-pouch. At the same time he looked the old gentleman steadily in the eye – a proceeding, as everybody knows, highly correct when maniacs are in question.

'Chilly,' Appleby said. 'But these gleams of sunshine are pleasant, all the same.'

The old gentleman appeared nonplussed. He even neglected to brandish his stick. Appleby took the opportunity to have a better look at him. He wondered why, if his dwelling had suggested some fabulous creature, he himself so strongly suggested a tortoise. He was thin, angular, and capable of at least a certain range of rapid nervous movements, so the image ought not to have fitted at all. Then Appleby remembered that tortoises are reputed to live for a very long time – the really big kinds for several centuries. And this is what the old gentleman gave the impression of doing. He looked by no means what could be called exceptionally old, but he did look as if he were engaged on the job of living almost indefinitely. It was a pervasive desiccation perhaps that rendered this impression; one felt that nothing could happen to his physical frame except – at some utterly remote future time – a slow crumbling and turning to dust. In a humbler walk of life he would be destined eventually to a booth in a fair, surrounded by impressive-looking documentary evidences of his extreme longevity, and offering to shake hands at sixpence a time.

This would have been an uncomfortable fancy in itself. But what made Appleby feel obscurely uneasy was his impression that the life thus suggesting itself as abnormally hardwearing and tenacious seemed also a life abnormally burdened after some nervous fashion. Here in fact was Pilgrim grown old with his bundle still on his back. It might be full of remorse and guilt and morbid scruple, as was the case with Bunyan's character. Or it might be full of the standard horrors of a modern psychiatric clinic: senseless obsessions, phobias, chasms of depression, self-hatred, despair.

The old gentleman had made no reply to Appleby's inane remark about the sunshine. He had simply stood in silence, watching him stuff his pipe. Something had changed in his manner, all the same. And this was signalized by the words – wholly surprising words – with which he greeted Appleby's first puff.

'What's that stuff you're smoking?'

'John Cotton 1 and 2.'

'I thought so.' The old gentleman hesitated. A new species of agitation appeared to have possessed him. 'I think I've got a pipe in the house,' he said.

'Then may we go and find it?' Appleby turned to walk on, but then paused until the old gentleman had come abreast of him. It was like dropping in on *Treasure Island* and coaxing Ben Gunn with an offer of Parmesan cheese. He wondered whether his host – as it suddenly seemed reasonable to term this curious old creature – was quite fantastically impoverished. The house they were now approaching certainly suggested it. So did the wild garden they had entered through a gate from the small park with its ill-repaired wall. Appleby took a cautious sideways glance at his companion. He wore a knickerbocker suit of antique cut. It was piped and patched at appropriate points with stout leather, and the cloth seemed of a quality that would last for ever anyway. The outfit might well have been tailored for the old gentleman's father round about the time of the Boer War. It carried a strong suggestion of the earliest days of cycling. Anything much in the way of shape had long since departed from it. But it was quite clean.

'My name is Ashmore,' the old gentleman said abruptly. He had come to a halt – and this time it was he who appeared to look Appleby steadily in the eye. If there was something wild in his gaze, there was something uncommonly penetrating as well. 'You've heard of me,' he said.

'I'm afraid I don't quite –' Appleby broke off. It was, he supposed, as a local magnate that the man called Ashmore presumed he must be known to his visitor. But the name rang only some faint and elusive bell. Unlike Judith, Appleby hadn't the knack of regarding anybody within fifteen miles as a close neighbour. If Judith had talked about this ancient Mr Ashmore as among the attractions of the neighbourhood her husband had been most culpably not listening to her. Nevertheless it was awkward to have to deny something that Ashmore had so dogmatically assumed, and Appleby was for a moment at a loss. Ashmore himself resumed the conversation.

'Don't think I'm a fool,' he said. 'Don't think I'm an old fool, or a bloody fool, or even just a born one. Didn't you say your name was Appleby, and talk about the police? I've placed you, you know. It's taken me a minute or two – but that doesn't mean my wits are wholly decayed. Mind you, they *may* be, but this isn't evidence of it. You've been an important man – Sir John, isn't it – but not *all* that important. So it takes a little thought to sort you out. And of course you've heard of me. Nobody in your position could have failed to.' Ashmore paused. 'Did you use to see those plays by that fellow Bernard Shaw?'

'Decidedly I did.'

'There's a man in one of them who goes around handing out his card. *Mr X, the Celebrated Coward.* Just like that. Well, I'm Martyn Ashmore, the celebrated ditto.' Ashmore laughed harshly. 'So now we are introduced. Can I have a fill of your tobacco, all the same?'

2

Judith – Appleby reflected – would have landed him in precisely this absurd situation. It was again the principle of going on till you are stopped. He recalled the occasion, for example, upon which she had insisted upon their 'exploring' – which meant simply breaking into – a house seemingly even more derelict and untenanted than this which confronted him now. There had been a moat round it, and owls had been appropriately hooting. It seemed incredible that any other human being had approached it for years. So they had climbed in through what had once been a window. They had hazardously ascended and descended tottering staircases. They had doubtfully distinguished on mouldering walls what had once been linenfold panelling. It had been great fun. And then the man had come. He was some sort of caretaker – an abandoned family retainer (they had afterwards decided) told off to prowl the place in order to repel such vulgar persons as might commit nuisances in corners or scratch initials or even more objectionable *graffiti* upon disgraced chimneypieces. They had heard his footfalls from afar. Footfalls plus an unnerving *tap*. For he was an ancient creature who got around only with the aid of a stick.

Plop, plop, and a *tap*. Plop, plop, and a *tap*. Admittedly it had been unnerving. Judith had persuaded him to hide in a cupboard.

Much later, and in an unwary moment, Appleby had told this story to the children. It must have been after dinner and when the Applebys – as tended to be their habit – were lingering amid Beaujolais and guttering candles before turning to at the washing-up. And now the story, if inexpugnably hilarious, had turned faintly tedious. The man, like some homing device of ghastly sophistication in modern warfare, had walked and tapped his way straight to the cupboard. He had thrown open the door – and there Sir John and Lady Appleby had been, like the woman (according to Bobby Appleby, who was of a literary turn) in a play of Strindberg's, who lived in a cupboard because she believed herself to be a parrot. And Appleby had emerged, fumbling for the famous visiting-card in one pocket while noisily jingling a kind of Danegeld of halfcrowns in the other. The man (according to Bobby) had behaved in an impeccably Jeeves-like manner. Recognizing (despite the halfcrowns, which had been a false note attributable to Appleby's unassuming origins) the presence of the upper classes, he had bowed the Applebys deferentially off the premises.

Bobby Appleby was not only of a literary turn. He had lately become a novelist. He was entitled to his fantasies. But *had* it been a fantasy? Appleby could no longer precisely remember. The cupboard indeed he could vividly recall. It had exuded what he vaguely conjectured to be the smell of the droppings of untold generations of bats. But had there really been that moment in which he had simultaneously obtruded an oblong of pasteboard (*Sir John Appleby, New Scotland Yard*) and a couple of halfcrowns? Appleby no longer knew. But he had been left with a distaste of what might be called false situations. Perhaps he was heading for one now.

The garden through which Mr Ashmore had conducted him abounded chiefly in hemlock and thistle – these (as once at Byron's Newstead) having choked up the rose that once bloomed on the spray. Here and there headless statues presided over exhausted fountains and departed shrubberies. There was a croquet-lawn abundant in fungi and mushrooms. Appleby rather suspected that Mr Ashmore relied upon these as upon a home farm; that the

fatally inviting stile had tumbled him into the society not
merely of a pathological recluse but of a pathological
miser as well. The mere possession of a tobacco-pouch had
transformed his status with the proprietor of this impressive if mouldering mansion. Extravagantly prosperous
gentlemen in the City of London would part with large
sums for the possession of so authentically feudal a set-up
as lay before him. But Mr Ashmore was prepared to admit
to it anybody who would provide him with a free smoke.

'I like your house very much,' Appleby said. 'I must
have missed it on my map. What is it called?'

'Ashmore Chase, of course.' Mr Ashmore had turned to
stare at him. 'What do you think? They're all around me,
my damned brothers and cousins in their bogus Lutyens
homes-and-gardens manor houses. Opening their interesting grounds for the benefit of District Nurses and God
knows what. But I'm the head of the family, after all. You
may say that the Sixteenth Century means nothing nowadays. Fair enough. But land does. I've been out in your
bloody modern world, and I've crashed in it. The Celebrated Coward and all that. But the estate's mine too.
And that's a different matter – eh? I know my rent-roll,
and I know their rotten stock-jobbing bubble-and-squeak
standing. No wonder they hate me. Well, I hate them
too.'

Appleby said nothing. These family amenities didn't
strike him as a very proper matter of communication to a
stranger. But he was surprised that he hadn't heard,
either from Judith or one of his new neighbours, of a
network of Ashmores in the county; he promised himself
to gain more accurate information about them than was
likely to come from the eccentric old person he was now
listening to. But he also wanted to know about the old
person's harping on the theme of the Celebrated Coward.
Just for the moment, he couldn't place this at all. He had
been challenged to respond to the name of Ashmore in a
way that in fact he couldn't do. When the old man had
said 'You've heard of me' some faint bell had indeed rung

in his head. But it hadn't, so to speak, rung up any curtain. Mr Ashmore owned some perished history which the world had cast into a deeper oblivion than he knew. Because curiosity had been so large a part of his professional life, Appleby had an instinct to get at this. But the time for it hadn't quite come. Perhaps it would come when the old fellow found that pipe.

But now it didn't look as if this was going to happen in a hurry. Mr Ashmore – Martyn Ashmore, as he had declared himself to be – appeared curiously reluctant to go indoors. They had reached a terrace which, although much overgrown, could be distinguished as attractively paved in ancient brick. This ran the length of the house on the front now exposed to them, and from it a few farther steps led up to a front door in equally ancient oak.

The door was shut. Apparently it was locked as well, for Ashmore as he walked up to it had produced from a pocket an impressively large key. Instead of applying this to the keyhole, however, he somewhat surprisingly applied his ear to it instead. Then, with a gesture to Appleby to follow him in silence, he moved softly down the terrace, pausing every now and then to peer cautiously through a window. But the windows were in so begrimed a state that this inspection could have had little practical utility, and Appleby was unable to resist an uncomfortable impression that what he was witnessing was a compulsive ritual devoid of rational significance. Presently they came to a second and smaller door of what appeared to be comparatively recent date, sheltered beneath a frankly unauthentic Gothic portico. This door – Appleby was further instructed to remark – was ajar and swaying gently to and fro in a light chilly breeze which was now rising. Ashmore paid no attention to it. He walked on to the next window, stopped, and anxiously examined its fastenings.

By this time it seemed evident to Appleby that there must be somebody around the place charged with the not very easy duty of looking after Mr Martyn Ashmore. Yet nobody of the sort had appeared – and for that matter he had been building up a strong impression that the old man lived in this great place in absolute solitude. He was about to frame a question which might throw some light on this when he saw that Ashmore had moved on.

But now they were approaching an angle of the house, and Ashmore's behaviour had become stranger still. He still held the big key in his hand – or rather he held it in both hands, cradling it as a trained Commando might cradle an automatic weapon. And some fantasy of this kind he actually went on to enact. As if this corner were a spot peculiarly vulnerable to a lethal enfilading fire, and with an agility altogether surprising in so elderly a man, he crouched, sprang and swung round the corner at the double. Appleby, caught unawares, found himself adopting a ludicrous compromise between the same manoeuvre and a more reasonable manner of circling a secluded country house on an unremarkable autumn day. He reflected impatiently that there was a great deal of Ashmore Chase; what had appeared at a first glance was that the house did nothing if not sprawl; this depressingly senile or demented war-game might go on for quite some time.

And this it did – to an extent indeed which prompted Appleby to ask a question the tone of which he a little regretted as he uttered it.

'May I ask whether you do this kind of thing often?'

For some moments Ashmore – who had started the window-business again – offered no reply, so that Appleby feared he must have offended him. But this proved to be not so, and Ashmore's answer when it came held almost the suggestion of polite conversation.

'Oh, dear me, no! Not at all. Only on the anniversary.'

'The anniversary?'

'Of their all being killed, of course. Massacred. Today is the anniversary. I told you, didn't I, that I remember the date?' Suddenly Martyn Ashmore looked strangely grim. 'I still have reason to.'

Suddenly Appleby quite definitely knew that he wanted to ask no more. Yet this, in some obscure way, was not possible. To close up when so strange a remark had been offered one would represent an indecent withdrawal of human sympathy. And he did feel a genuine if still wholly uncomprehending sympathy with this strangely driven recluse. He waited however until the ritual dash round a further wing of the house had been made.

'I'm afraid I don't quite understand you. Do you mean that there is one special day in the year in which you face a peculiar physical hazard?'

'Just that. They make an attempt upon my life only on the one day. And, even so, only one single attempt. It's a matter of their honour. Too much honour – honour and dishonour – about the whole thing.'

'Why don't you keep yourself securely shut away on this one dangerous day of the year? Or call in the police? It ought to be quite easy.'

'I funked once. I gave in once. No good came of it. Did you ever read *Nostromo* by the fellow Conrad? Some sort of foreigner.'

'I've read it more than once, as a matter of fact.'

'Dr Monygham. A gentleman – English gentleman. He gave in. It broke him.'

'It didn't break him. He ends up as the voice of reason and morality in the book. But why did you give in?'

'They had an electrical thing. After some hours I couldn't take it any longer. I show you the places – if they were at all decent.'

Appleby acknowledged a long silence. They had now got right round the house. Its front door was again ahead of them. The day seemed to have darkened – to have turned suddenly colder, as is said to happen when ghosts walk. Appleby knew that he must speak again.

'Something very bad followed?'

'The whole village. The men were shot. The women and children were told to go and pray for their souls in the church. Then they fired it. I was made to watch.' The crazed country gentleman called Martyn Ashmore was silent again for a time. 'It wouldn't have been quite so bad, you know, if my mother hadn't been French.'

'But even in the years immediately after that sort of thing happened, surely, people didn't exact vengeance from men who ... who were tortured until they talked.'

'It wasn't believed. It was thought to be a put-up job. Don't blame them. Collaboration often worked like that.'

'Good God, man!' In the stillness of the early afternoon Appleby heard his own voice almost crying out. 'This must have been nearly thirty years ago! You can't believe –'

Ashmore made no direct reply. He walked up to the front door, and this time put the key in the lock without hesitation. He turned it, threw open the door, and stepped back as if to let Appleby be the first to enter.

'I hope,' he said, 'you'll stay to lunch.'

It was in this second that the thing happened. Suddenly between the two men the worn brick on which they stood quivered and seemed to explode. There was a crash and an effect of flying splinters. There was a brief dust. A large flat stone – a roofing stone – lay in fragments at their feet.

Appleby looked up. He saw a mouldering and crenellated parapet. Behind it there must lie a flat leaded space. Beyond that rose the swell of the ancient roof from which this deadly projectile must have come. He was instantly and enormously angry. Martyn Ashmore had been within inches of his end. So for that matter had been a retired and inoffensive Commissioner of Metropolitan Police. He grabbed Ashmore and dragged him within the shelter of the doorway.

'Have you servants?' he demanded. 'Have you a telephone?'

'A telephone? Yes, of course. But they've disconnected it. The post-office people. They were demanding some extortionate rent.'

Appleby scarcely heard this. He was listening to something else—the sound of flying feet on what must be an uncarpeted staircase. He dashed into a gloomy hall. A door banged. He turned towards the noise, but its direction eluded him. Then from somewhere beyond the back of the house came the roar of a motor-cycle engine. It rose and then rapidly faded into distance.

'Another failure,' Ashmore said. 'Three hundred and sixty-five days to go.' He laughed harshly, but his voice was steady. 'And now about luncheon. Would claret or burgundy be your choice?'

It was not much Appleby's habit, in any crisis, to lose a tolerably sharp consciousness of his surroundings. But he was forced afterwards to admit that it was in an almost dreamlike state that he had traversed shabby and almost empty rooms, had watched his host light a candle, had descended behind him into just such a cellar as he had fatuously imagined he might be incarcerated in by a maniac. It wasn't an empty cellar. He opened his eyes wide, indeed, at what he saw.

'What about this?' Ashmore was asking, and held up a bottle.

'That's brandy,' Appleby said. Even in this extraordinary situation he was able to reflect that it was a long time since he had set eyes on just such a bottle – its neck bulbous with wax, its label hand-written in France long ago.

'Yes, of course.' Ashmore put the brandy back in its rack. 'We want a half-bottle, wouldn't you say?' His impulse of hospitality seemed to be moderating itself. 'One doesn't care to turn too sleepy of an afternoon, eh? And here they are. Lafite.' His unnerving laugh echoed queerly beneath the vaulting of the chilly place. 'You must try my Lafite. Just a glass.'

3

The wine was superb, but only the most evil-hearted of grocers could have purveyed the cheese. Appleby ate it heartily all the same – mostly with the end of a knife, since the bread available at Ashmore Chase was on the elderly side. He found that the morning's adventure had given him an appetite, and this he took to be a sign that there remained to him at least some vestige of the spirit of youth. In a sense however it was an adventure wasted on him; he had spent too much of his life walking in and out of affairs of this sort; the thing would have come at least with a greater effect of impact to another man: a quietly wayfaring scholar, say, or the simplest of citizens on a country jaunt. On the other hand he was himself at least in a strong position to get on with the matter, since he need waste no time in perturbation or amazement.

And certainly he couldn't simply let it lie. It had undeniably become his affair, since one can't see either oneself or another within inches of being murdered and at once merely close the file. Moreover there seemed something helpless and unprotected in Martyn Ashmore's situation which had the effect of placing additional responsibility upon even the most fortuitously contacted representative of society and the law. That this went with something courageous in the man – that although a rum old creature with some unknown horror behind him he was yet evidently indisposed to flap – seemed no more than a fact constituting an additional claim.

And the first point was clear. Something extremely definite had *happened*. At one moment, that was to say, Appleby had been supposing himself in the presence of a harmless eccentric – or lunatic, to use a harsher word. In the next moment an event had *happened* which had at least served to set the old gentleman's outlandish behaviour in some rational consonance with outer reality. The stone that had come crashing down in that transforming instant might fairly be called a sizeable chunk of just that: outer reality in its most lethal form.

It hadn't come down by accident. It hadn't come down as a mere alarming joke. The person who dropped it had aimed it – and had surely been curiously indifferent as to which of the two figures below got killed. Or had the assailant so concentrated on Ashmore that he (or she) simply failed to notice Appleby standing within a few feet of him? It didn't seem possible. What was perhaps worth remarking was the fact that probability had remained a little against anybody getting killed at all. It had been a murderous attack conducted, so to speak, on the principles of Russian roulette. If Ashmore himself was to be believed – which there was no very compelling evidence to persuade one to do – something of this sort happened to him precisely once a year, and obscurely as the consequence of a bygone horror so hideously hinted that Appleby's scepticism had faltered before it. Yet even if one granted that Ashmore had experienced some unspeakable outrage, direr still in its consequences, in occupied France, it didn't necessarily follow that either the hurtled stone or (if they really had happened) any of its annual equivalents were in the causal relationship with those distant events that Ashmore supposed them to be.

Appleby finished his cheese. It was definitely mouldy. He finished his claret. It was faintly musty, as the most perfect clarets are. He didn't delude himself that the facts he had just been reviewing made the faintest sense in his head. But he still felt that action was required of him. Even if – fantastically – it was true that Ashmore's life would not again be in danger until a year had elapsed it didn't mean that a resolute attempt ought not to be made to catch here and now the person who had ridden away on a motor-cycle.

Appleby felt he had already been remiss about this. But the trouble lay in Ashmore's attitude to his guest, which was bewilderingly fluctuating and inconsequent. At present he was pleasing himself – living in this pathologically miserly and reclusive manner as he did – in dredging up as from some former existence the attitudes of an urbane and practised host, entertaining a neighbouring gentleman amid all the amenities of a well-appointed establishment. The wartime episode, the mysterious annual persecution, its latest exemplification at the very door of Ashmore Chase an hour ago: these topics had somehow become taboo during the frugal repast. It wasn't at all clear to Appleby how Ashmore would receive a proposal to turn to and prosecute a little detective investigation on the spot. Nevertheless the proposal must be made.

'I've very much enjoyed my lunch,' Appleby said. 'And now – do you know? – I'd rather like to climb up and have a look at your roof. And perhaps at the back of the house as well.'

'My dear sir, I shall be delighted. These would not be my own first choice, and perhaps you will permit me to show you a little more of the house. It is an unassuming place, but at least I can act the cicerone with affection. But you must check me, if I too much indulge in family history.'

'I don't think I shall do that.' Following his host's example, Appleby rose from table – a plain scrubbed table, for they had eaten in a kitchen. 'Your family history would interest me very much.'

'My poor father, Ayden Ashmore,' Ashmore said, and paused.

They were traversing, at the top of one wing of the house, a long gallery – a gallery indeed not all that long, yet answering respectably to one's idea of this characteristic apartment in a Jacobean mansion. The portrait was that of a young man in his mid-twenties, and Appleby was less immediately struck by his features than by his attire.

'In fancy dress?' he ventured.

'Nothing of the kind.' Martyn Ashmore stared. 'The portrait is by Haydon – Benjamin Robert Haydon.'

'Haydon?' It was Appleby's turn to stare. 'But Haydon painted Wordsworth! He even painted Keats, who died –'

'Oh, no doubt. But he also painted gentlemen as well.' Ashmore, as he achieved this magnificent piece of cross-purposes, shook his head sadly before the young man in his late-Georgian finery. 'My poor father's life was a tragedy.'

'I am very sorry to hear it.' Appleby, with improbable sums in his head, looked speculatively at his host. 'At least he can scarcely have died young.'

'He died in a hunting accident. It was in his ninety-ninth year, when he was already preparing for his small family celebration. It cut me up very much. I was a lad of eight at the time.' Ashmore moved on. 'Perhaps it *is* a shade surprising. But it just so happens that, in my family, there is a tradition of marrying a little late. May I invite your attention to this by Charles Jarvis? It is of my grandfather Silas.'

'And Jarvis painted another of the English poets, Alexander Pope.' Appleby recalled his reflections on the life-rhythm of the tortoise. He had scarcely been wrong about its relevance to his new acquaintance.

'Of course,' Martyn Ashmore was saying, 'Jarvis painted my grandfather when he was still an Eton boy. You can see that. My grandfather was born in 1720. He was known among his familiars, even to the end of his long life, as "Bubbles" Ashmore. It was the year, you know, of the South Sea Bubble.'

'I suppose your grandfather married rather late in life too?' Appleby followed up this harmless question with one which he felt, even as he uttered it, to be impertinent. 'And perhaps you may carry on the tradition?'

'It's a question which others are asking themselves.' Ashmore, who seemed unoffended, produced a malicious chuckle as he said this. 'But I think you mentioned the roof? There is a point of access to it above the front door. But I am afraid that it affords no very great extension of view.'

Appleby found himself walking on – and presently descending some stairs and ascending others – in a meditative silence. About the Ashmores he was obliged, he supposed, to believe what he had been told. Perhaps Martyn Ashmore was a little embroidering or overstating the facts; perhaps he had even skipped a generation in his leapfrogging progress back to the age of Queen Anne; but notable longevity and a propensity to take up the task of procreation only at an advanced age no doubt ran in his family authentically enough. What was perplexing was the manner in which, while airing these matters, he seemed entirely to have dismissed both the dreadful personal history at which he had hinted and the sufficiently startling event of an hour ago – which he had declared to be only one in a series of such events with which that history continued to implicate him annually.

Perhaps he had an iron nerve, so that what occasioned him a very natural anxiety in the immediate prospect he was at once able to banish from his mind as soon as he was assured of his next twelve months' immunity. Or perhaps he simply suffered from some disorder of the memory, so that his mental life was subject to pathological discontinuities. If, after all, he had suffered what he had so briefly claimed to have suffered, and seen what he had equally briefly claimed to have seen, then he surely had some title to be a little off his head. And if furthermore – beyond all sober belief as it seemed – he was in fact the recurrent object of a species of diabolically cat-and-mouse revenge, then equally surely he could claim credit for not being vastly madder still.

But now they had climbed a final flight of wooden steps – it was little more than a ladder with a handrail – and passed through a low door. They were in open air, with a flat leaded area beneath their feet, the long spine of a steeply pitched stone roof behind them, and in front a low parapet constituted by battlements of a conventional sort. They were not particularly high up, since the house nowhere rose above two main storeys and a range of attic rooms. Appleby walked to the battlements and looked over. What lay immediately below was undoubtedly the front door. Ashmore had at least brought him straight to the spot from which the attack had been launched. And this seemed good enough warrant for recurring to it.

'These periodic attempts to murder you,' Appleby said boldly. 'Do you regard them as strictly your own affair, or have you been accustomed to report them to the police?'

'Oh, that!' Ashmore's tone, if not exactly dismissive, was that of a man to whom a topic of no great moment has been proposed. 'I don't make a fuss.'

'You must forgive me for appearing merely curious. I realize the thing is no business of mine.'

'Not at all.' Ashmore turned to Appleby decisively. 'Here you are, my dear sir, consenting to be my guest – and after some initial misunderstanding which I regret. And as a result, somebody nearly brains you. I say just enough – or so I suppose – to explain the matter, and pass to less disagreeable topics. But you are certainly entitled to a further word, if you feel that way. What's that about the police? You told me you were a policeman yourself. Indeed, I've heard of you, as I said. Am I to understand that you are acting –'

'Nothing of the kind, Mr Ashmore. I have no standing in your affair whatever. Perhaps I'm talking entirely out of turn. What happened before lunch stemmed, you say, from some very painful incident in the past. I do confess to wondering whether that fact has prompted you to keep quite mum about these attempts, or whether the local police know about them.'

'I don't see the local police doing much about them. Outside their range, if you ask me.'

'I must disagree with you.' Appleby spoke more forcibly than he had yet ventured to do. 'If it is really true that your life is in some danger on only one day of the year, it is evident that the police could ensure your absolute safety upon it with very little inconvenience to either themselves or you.'

'I think you said earlier that I could manage that off my own bat. I refuse to disarrange my life over the matter. But I may as well tell you that the police *do* know about it. At least their Chief Constable does.'

'Colonel Pride?'

'That's right – young Tommy Pride. I've mentioned it to him more than once when meeting him in a casual way. At drinks somewhere or other – that sort of thing. I don't, as a matter of fact, go around very much nowadays. I might almost be called a bit of a recluse, you know. But there are three or four neighbours on whom I have a kind of duty to drop in just occasionally. Trouble is, I'm so liable to meet some of my damned relations. Cursed number of Ashmores round these parts.'

This, Appleby recalled, was a note which his host had already sounded. At the moment it seemed a red herring, and he had better stick to the Chief Constable.

'And what action,' he asked, 'did Colonel Pride think it best to take?'

'Oh, he didn't take any action! I wasn't urging anything on him, you know. It seemed to me proper he should be put in the picture, eh? But I wasn't crying out. Thought I'd made that point with you.'

'You made it, all right.' Standing on what must have been the precise spot from which that deadly stone had been dropped or flung, Appleby scrutinized the owner of Ashmore Chase anew. Then he thought of the Chief Constable. Colonel Pride had in recent months become quite well known to him, and although there might be aspects of police work in which this gallant soldier was distinguishably an amateur Appleby made no question of his being a thoroughly conscientious person. If he had taken no action as a result of Martyn Ashmore's story it could only be because Ashmore had so told his story as to give the strongest impression of being gently mad. Pride of course had not enjoyed the additional stimulus to action of seeing a sizeable chunk of stone suddenly fragment itself in the vicinity of his feet. Appleby promised himself to relay his own persuasive experience to Pride as rapidly as might be. Pride was not perhaps to be described as an Appleby enthusiast, but he had accepted amiably enough the rather tiresome bobbing up in his neighbourhood of a superannuated top policeman from London. He would certainly not be disposed to assert that Appleby had been imagining things.

Quite possibly, with the ordinary resources of a detective branch, this deplorable affair could be got to the bottom of almost at once. Failing that, it should be easy to ensure that a year today (whether with Ashmore's knowledge or not) a disagreeable reception should be awaiting anybody making a felonious approach to Ashmore Chase. Appleby found himself looking forward to this with satisfaction. It was odd how angry he still felt. Often enough in the past, desperation of one sort or another had prompted various people to deliberate attempts on his life. He couldn't recall ever having been furious about it. There must be something particularly exacerbating in being nearly killed as the mere consequence of a casual encounter during a blameless country walk.

Meanwhile, he wondered whether an old professional instinct could be aroused in Ashmore as well as in himself. If what Ashmore had recounted was true, tragedy had come to him only as a result of his being in some situation which an active and adventurous man could alone find himself in; the background of his story appeared to be the *Résistance* in occupied France. It should be possible to coax him into a mood in which his

30

reaction to danger and violence would be other than his present mask (if it was that) of contemptuous disregard.

'Why a stone from your own roof?' Appleby demanded suddenly. He turned and pointed. 'I know about that sort of construction, and I'm sure you do too. It's immemorial, and it's made to last. One might be able to wrench one of these heavy slabs free, but one couldn't reckon on it. Why didn't he bring something handier up with him? Did he want to suggest an accident?'

'Perhaps *you* want to suggest an accident.' Suddenly Ashmore's attention did really seem engaged, and he pointed in his turn. 'It could have been an accident – if the stone had simply become detached from somewhere up there near the ridge of the roof. By the time it reached this flat platform its momentum might be such as to bounce it over the parapet. That's it, isn't it – and all the rest just an old fellow imagining things?'

'To be frank, I rather wish that it was – since your story, you know, is an uncommonly uncomfortable one.' Appleby smiled disarmingly. 'Unfortunately it just isn't so. A sharp-edged stone crashing down on this lead might conceivably bounce, but it would leave a substantial gash or scar in doing so. I wouldn't believe it to have been an accident even if I hadn't heard that motor-cycle. Besides, you know, the stone *didn't* come from high up. It came from *there*.' Appleby's finger went out straight in front of him. 'Right by the fellow's hand.'

There could be no doubt of it. A slab had successfully been wrenched from the roof, and the underlying stone thus uncovered was lighter in colour than those surrounding it, so that what had happened was visible at once. Appleby walked up to the place. He had to inspect it only for a moment before suddenly stiffening. Then he turned to his companion. 'I think you may feel you know,' he said, 'just how to interpret *that*?'

That was a very simple design which had been boldly

scratched on the exposed surface with a sharp instrument:

For a moment both men looked at this in silence. Appleby recorded to himself an impression that Martyn Ashmore's breathing was for the moment not perfectly regular. But when the old man spoke it was detachedly and with a faint irony.

'Perhaps it isn't as recent as it looks? A mason's mark, would you say? They were still very fond of them in the sixteenth century.'

'No doubt.' Appleby's tone indicated that he took no pleasure in this trifling. 'But if that is a medieval stonemason's mark, Mr Ashmore, what he chose to sign himself with was the Cross of Lorraine. It was to have other associations in a later age.'

4

The breeze which had begun to blow earlier was still rising, and it made the present perch of Appleby and his host a chilly one. It was beginning to whistle in the battlements – and also to sigh subtly or whisper in the innumerable small crevices of the ancient roof. Appleby's last words had been followed by a silence in which he had believed himself to be listening only to these murmurings of external nature. But now he suddenly raised his head and listened in another fashion.

'Can there be anybody else up here?' he asked. 'Somebody who for some reason came up before us? I haven't gathered whether you have many servants about the place.'

'Servants?' Ashmore produced a contemptuous exclamation. 'I do without them entirely, praise the Lord! Do you know the kind of wages they ask for nowadays? Totally impossible!'

'Yes, of course.' Appleby was still listening. At the same time he was reflecting that, as the owner of what was clearly a substantial estate in this particular part of England, Martyn Ashmore, regardless of other sources of wealth, could not be other than an extremely prosperous man. Indeed he had himself hinted as much. Of a thoroughly irrational element in his parsimony there could be no doubt whatever.

'But I think you're right,' Ashmore said. He had cocked his head on one side in an attitude of listening. But if this somehow enhanced the effect of an unnatural agelessness in his features – rather as if a death-mask had been canted over on its stand – it also suggested an almost unimpaired capacity for alert attention to his surroundings when he was minded that way. His senses, Appleby thought, had remained with him more certainly than his wits. And now he turned to Appleby and nodded. 'Not a doubt of it.'

Appleby surveyed their situation. Even the principal façade of the house was without regularity, and one consequence of this was apparent at their present level. On their left hand as they faced outwards towards the park the battlemented effect abruptly left off, so that the roof-structure terminated merely in impassable eaves and a gutter. But on their right a cheerfully incongruous Gothicizing had been carried out, with the result that there were more battlements, and a narrow leaded walk behind them. Along this one could move in very reasonable safety. The route would take one round a corner of the roof. And it was from this direction that something like the sound of footfalls had come.

'Nobody can have slipped up behind us,' Appleby said. 'If there's anybody there, he's been up here for some time. If you don't mind, we'll go and have a look.'

But this proposal proved unnecessary. Even as Appleby spoke, the figure of a man appeared round the angle of the roof, hesitated for a moment before what he saw, and then advanced upon them with what was almost an air of leisure. He was quite a young man, in clothes so expressive of English casual elegance that one instantly conjectured him to be a foreigner. And confirmation of this appeared in the first words he spoke.

'*Mille pardons!*' the young man said – and as he spoke his glance travelled between Appleby and Ashmore, as if he were rapidly sorting them out. It was to Ashmore that he now made an expressive gesture. '*Je suis très, très confus,*' he said.

And he smiled with an easy charm which, on the contrary, didn't in the least suggest embarrassment.

It was in French that the young man continued for some minutes to explain himself. Appleby missed out a little on the beginning of this; his French was very adequate, but in face of really fast bowling, so to speak, he commonly took some time to play himself in. And the young man talked with a volubility which at the same time had the precision of well-bred speech; he didn't appear to be in any doubt that Ashmore at least would follow him easily. It was when Appleby recalled Ashmore's claiming – during that sinister recital – to have had a French mother, indeed, that what was being said now started to be fully intelligible. The young man's name was Jules de Voisin; he had the happiness to be a kinsman of Mr Ashmore's; he had come to pay his respects to one whose name was so much honoured in his own family.

Appleby as he listened to this took a swift glance at Martyn Ashmore – Martyn Ashmore who like the man in Shaw's play called himself the Celebrated Coward. His disaster would have been more bearable, he had said, had his mother *not* been French. Appleby glanced back at Jules de Voisin. Was it possible that his visit was malignly motivated, and that in his last speech there had lurked some vicious irony? Was it even possible –

Appleby abandoned speculation so as not to let his French slip again. Monsieur de Voisin had come to the tricky part of his explanation – and if he saw the hurdle to be a high one he nevertheless took it like a bird. The house having appeared for the moment untenanted, he had reflected that here after all was the dwelling of a *parent*. And having chanced to come upon a side-door hospitably ajar, he had ventured simply to enter – not indeed to commit the impertinence of freely roaming the mansion, but simply in the hope of what he had in fact achieved: ascending to some point of vantage from which he could comprehensively survey those *parterres, vergers* and *potagers* – not to speak of *le parc bien boisé* – which had so delighted him as he made his approaches through his honoured kinsman's *domaine*. And having said so much in a language eminently suited to refined compliment, young Monsieur de Voisin suddenly switched to the most colloquial English – this to admit his better sense that it really all had been the most tremendous cheek.

Mr Ashmore distinguishably felt it to have been that – and so did Appleby. The French are a people rather formally disposed, and this young man's behaviour could scarcely be viewed as other than odd. But Ashmore didn't greet the outrageous intrusion with anything like the ire he had allowed himself at Appleby's much more harmless trespass a couple of hours earlier. In fact he was detectably rather at a loss. It was as if the visitor had confronted him with a problem he couldn't yet confidently assess. Was it conceivable that the turning up of a real Frenchman was stirring in Ashmore an uneasy knowledge that certain other Frenchmen existed only inside his own head?

'May I ask,' Appleby said suddenly, 'whether you are running around on a motor-bicycle?'

For an instant de Voisin seemed to hesitate, and then sufficiently accounted for this by a gesture suggesting that here had been an idiom he hadn't at once understood. Which was fair enough, Appleby thought. The English language does play itself odd tricks.

'But, ah – no!' De Voisin made a further gesture conceivably indicating a politely dissimulated consciousness that his kinsman's friend had addressed him without the formality of introduction. 'I have my little car. But not here at the house, since I left it at the entrance to the drive. The walk through the grounds was too charming to miss.'

Appleby accepted this in silence. The young man was much overdoing, he thought, the picturesque charms of Ashmore Chase, since the decidedly run-down character of its pleasure gardens and policies in general would surely be anybody's predominant impression of it. But Gallic politeness, no doubt, had still to be allowed for.

'But I did observe a motor-cyclist,' de Voisin went on. 'He came up the drive and out of the park just as I was entering it.' The young man paused, as if aware of himself as being surprisingly informative. He continued with precision nevertheless. 'That was at twenty to two, just as I began my *promenade*. But I have not been here so long as that would suggest, since I made my small picnic *en route*.'

'I see. You were mistaken, by the way, in supposing this house to be empty as well as accessible. Mr Ashmore and I must have been at lunch when you entered.'

Jules de Voisin received this communication only with a bow. It was, Appleby reflected, a perfectly justifiable snub. If Martyn Ashmore was indisposed to indicate overt displeasure at his French kinsman's behaviour it certainly wasn't for a casual guest to do so. Nevertheless Appleby was suddenly determined to have nothing whatever swept, so to speak, under the mat.

'I congratulate you,' he said, 'on being so certain of just when you saw the motor-cycle. It may be a point of importance. There can be little doubt that its rider must be regarded as a dangerous criminal. In fact he attempted to murder Mr Ashmore not much more than an hour ago from this very spot.'

Naturally enough, de Voisin received this with a shocked exclamation. He then turned to Martyn Ashmore and appeared to indicate by a raised eyebrow his continuing sense of the irregular character of this conversation.

'Sir John Appleby,' Ashmore said. 'Another new acquaintance, my dear – um – Jules. But a neighbour, more or less. Sir John has held a very distinguished position. You may think of him as having been *Préfet de Police* in London. Appleby, my kinsman, Jules de Voisin.'

Appleby was more impressed by this performance than de Voisin appeared to be. It indicated considerable reserves of clarity in his eccentric host. It even seemed to sanction Appleby's taking to himself a certain professional standing in relation to the homicidal incident he had just referred to. But if de Voisin was surprised he failed to show it. Having, with a relapse into his native tongue, announced that he was enchanted to make Appleby's acquaintance, he surveyed the small platform on which all three men stood with the decently enhanced interest proper to its having been revealed as the scene of recent outrage. With an equally becoming gravity he felicitated his kinsman on his fortunate escape from danger. He then again fell silent. It was a silence which conveyed that he was by no means dismissing without further concern the startling information he had been offered. Its implication seemed rather to be that further discussion of it ought to be a family affair, and not to take place in the presence of Sir John Appleby – *Préfet de Police*, or not.

It was again, Appleby judged, fair enough. It wasn't clear to him, all the same, that he ought now simply to take his leave – not even if it was to carry the whole story at once to Colonel Pride. For it was not credible, after all, that there wasn't something to be discovered about this young Frenchman in some way relevant to the plain crime that had been attempted. That he should have turned up by sheer coincidence on a kinsman he had never before set eyes on precisely on the day which had seen that kinsman's attempted murder was too improbable for any ready belief; it would have been so even if Ashmore had not himself provided that attempt with an obscure but lurid French background. Appleby decided at least to make one more exploratory move.

'You ought to know something of the circumstances,' he said to de Voisin. 'They represent an odd mingling of premeditation and improvisation. Or that's the appearance of the thing. The fellow ensconced himself here, and lay in wait until Mr Ashmore (as it happened, in my company) came up to his front door – which is directly beneath, as you can see. A shot would have settled the matter. But he employed something just a little less accurate. He yanked a stone —'

'Yanked?'

'He wrenched a stone from the roof, and dropped or lobbed it over this parapet.' Appleby paused. 'Would you care to see where it came from?'

De Voisin was again – in effect – *enchanté*; he evinced, in other words, a purely conventional interest. Or this was how he appeared. But then de Voisin – Appleby inclined to conclude – was rather a deep young man. Perhaps he was at once deep and out of his depth. Or perhaps – but this was highly speculative – he was playing it all a little more cool than was perfectly *convenable* simply because what he had stumbled upon was in some way wholly staggering.

'You can see where one stone is missing,' Appleby said. 'If you consider that a full half of it was tucked away beneath the row immediately above, you'll see that it can't have been very easy to prise out – and that it was big enough to brain an elephant ... Take a closer look, Monsieur de Voisin.'

Rather as one courteously acquiescent before some importunate invitation to view an uninteresting knick-knack, heirloom, or indeed mere snapshot, de Voisin did as he was required. Perhaps he was a little short-sighted, for a fraction of a second seemed to pass before he became aware of the enigmatically scratched surface of the freshly exposed stone. When he did so he gave a startled exclamation. But when he turned to Appleby it was with an expression at once of anger and of contempt. And it was very deliberately that he spoke in his own tongue.

'*Je ne le crois pas, Monsieur. C'est un galimatias, une pure bêtise.*'

In the silence which for a moment followed this the rising wind continued to murmur and whisper in the interstices of the roof. According to one's mood, one might have concluded the effect to be either maleficent or benign; a sinister stirring of those natural forces by which the pyramids themselves will one day be worn away, or a comfortable cradle song crooned by earth over a structure which, although venerable to a human eye, must nestle in a mere infancy to the eye of time.

But if Appleby had been disposed to poetical reflection of this sort – which he was not – he would certainly have been recalled from it by the curious behaviour of his host. If de Voisin was oddly angered by what he had seen, his English relative was yet more angered by what he had heard – by the scornful exclamation, that is to say, which the young Frenchman had produced upon becoming aware of the scrawled Cross of Lorraine. But Martyn Ashmore was not merely indignant; he was agitated as well. He had become in fact very much the Ashmore into whose arms Appleby had more or less tumbled over the stile. It was almost as if something which was essentially a protective fantasy were under attack.

And now, for the first time, Ashmore spoke in French. He spoke so vehemently, and was so instantly answered by his young visitor in a similar key – for seconds indeed to an effect of shouting one another down – that Appleby's ear was again momentarily baffled. Then this indecorous episode ended as abruptly as it had begun. Ashmore had pulled himself up – and although his limbs were trembling his voice had come wholly under control. He turned to Appleby.

'My dear Sir John, you will realize that it is a long time since I have received a visit from one of my French connections. It is a red-letter day, and I find myself becoming positively excited! I take it very kindly that Jules should have made his way to the Chase. I rather fear his visit may be only a short one. And he and I, as you may imagine, will have plenty of family matters to talk about.'

'That will be most agreeable, I don't doubt.' Appleby glanced curiously at de Voisin, hoping for some indication of how he felt about this belated welcome. But de Voisin merely returned the glance with faint irony. He had entirely picked up the abruptness with which Appleby had been dismissed.

It was a dismissal to take gracefully. Appleby murmured further words about his excellent lunch, shook hands solemnly with both men, and begged to be so far indulged as to see himself out of the house. Mr Ashmore and Monsieur de Voisin, he added, would no doubt wish to spend a little more time admiring the view.

In five minutes he was walking thoughtfully down a weed-covered drive. Tentatively, he tried telling himself that what lay behind him was no affair of his. But he found it wouldn't do. Simply as a matter of public duty it wouldn't do. He would run over that evening, he decided, and have a word with the Chief Constable.

Part Two

Benevolent Intentions at Long Dream Manor

5

'Do you mean,' Judith Appleby asked, 'that you went on till you were stopped?'

'Precisely that. I observed your canons in such matters to the letter.' Appleby accepted a second cup of tea, shook his head austerely at a seducing plate of chocolate Bath Olivers, and then nodded it in gloomy substantiation of what he had just said. 'And no good came of it. No good ever does.'

'It doesn't strike me that way at all.' Judith, whose weight remained constant regardless of dietary indulgence, picked up one of the biscuits. 'You arrived home with a mystery – or at least with the tip or the ghost of a mystery – and you've been battening on it ever since. All that business, for example, of rushing over to alarm poor Tommy Pride. You enjoy it enormously. Just like old times. Much better fun than stacking wood. By the way, we'll be out of dry wood and living in a smoky house before Christmas if you don't –'

'Very well.' Appleby gave a decisive nod. 'I'll tell Hoobin.'

'Yes, do tell Hoobin, John. And don't forget his bottle of whisky. It will be for his eightieth birthday.'

'Of course not.' Appleby gave a resigned sigh. 'Your hale and hearty husband will go through this Caliban act, stacking wood. And the octogenarian Hoobin, a dignified Prospero, will tipple whisky in the potting shed. What were we talking about?'

'*The Great Maquis Mystery*. Or perhaps *Peril at Ashmore Chase*. And about scaring Tommy Pride.'

'I'm not in the least averse to scaring Tommy Pride. I

wasn't at school with him. I didn't dance with him at hunt balls, as you –'

'Of course not. Men don't do that sort of thing at hunt balls. Or not at the balls of *good* hunts.'

'You are quite idiotic. I am only saying that I don't mind scaring your Tommy. Not that it *is* scaring him. Pride's a very good scout. As for the *maquis*, it's not to be joked about. In France itself such things went on happening for years after the war. A fellow would square this chap and that, and get himself solemnly acquitted in court of any species of collaboration. And then young men – or not so young men – who had acquired a taste for summary justice under *résistance* rules would turn up one night and simply rub him out. Read *Les Mandarins*. Simone de Beauvoir, you know.'

'I *do* know. But they didn't fall down on the job every 10th of October.'

'Fair enough.' Appleby got up and paced the room. 'There's something really fiendish in that. It's as if they want to break his nerve – just as it was once broken by some hideous secret police long ago. So far, it looks as if this old man – who *is* an old man, and destined by some freak of heredity to go on getting yet older for a long time – allows himself to get worried for about twenty-four hours in the year. They want *really* to get him down. And then, I suppose, they'll end up that series of near-misses, and contrive a square hit. It's not at all nice. I didn't scare Pride, but I'm glad to think I've alerted him. He feels he may have rather rashly discounted this Martyn Ashmore's seemingly incredible yarn. He's making inquiries. As a matter of fact I expect him to drop in this evening.'

'John, do you *believe* this fantastic tale?'

'I believe in that hunk of stone. And so would you, my dear, if you'd felt the wind of it on your left ear.'

'I believe in it too.' Judith looked seriously at her husband. There had been plenty of times when she had sat over two poached eggs round about 9 p.m., trying not to wonder whether she would ever see John again. She didn't like this story of sudden and insane danger during a day's ramble from Long Dream. 'But I don't at all know what to believe about your young Frenchman. Of course it's true that Martyn Ashmore has French relations.'

'His father married a de Voisin?'

'His father – Ayden Ashmore – married ages ago a *bonne bourgeoise* called Annette Dupont. Very much the *haute bourgeoisie*, as they say. Related to all sorts of people, however, with much grander names.'

'How you contrive –'

'I knew some of them when I was almost finished for good at that ghastly French school. Before I ran away to the Slade. Before I met my glorious policeman.'

'No doubt.' Appleby sat down again, and with conscious complacency finished his tea. 'And you also know all about this rash of Ashmores who appear to be our near neighbours at the other end of the county. I think I'll want to know about them too ... Judith, why aren't you listening to me?'

'Of course I'm listening to you.' But Lady Appleby's ear had been quite detectably attuned to the outer world. 'But Bobby's coming for the week-end. I thought I heard what might be his car.'

'Fine. You'll be able to talk to him about Simone de Beauvoir.'

'Bobby thinks the Beaver and Sartre and all that fearfully old-hat. Bobby belongs to the *anti-roman* school. What he goes in for is called *la nouvelle écriture*.'

'He hasn't given up hope of educating me.' Appleby picked up a book. 'I've been told to read this, by a chap called Alain Robbe-Grillet. It's described as a novel, but a great deal of it seems just to be describing a house. The first paragraph is about a veranda. Listen. *Since its width is the same for the central portion as for the sides, the line of shadow cast by the column extends precisely to the corner of the house; but it stops there, for only the*

*veranda flagstones are reached by the sun ... At this
moment the shadow of the outer edge of the roof co-
incides exactly with the right angle formed by the
terrace and the two vertical surfaces of the corner of
the house.'* Appleby put down the book. 'Odd, don't you
think?'

'It ought to appeal to you. It's by rather an observing
kind of person.'

'That's undeniable.' Forgetting about Monsieur Robbe-
Grillet, Appleby walked to the window. He too was
hearkening to the outer world. He was commonly as
relieved as Judith when their youngest child's alarming
car was heard to come safely to a stop in the drive. Bobby
Appleby had once been a useful youth in the middle of
the front row of a scrum. He had then surprisingly transformed himself into an even more useful scrum-half. In
that position he had played a very decent game against
the All Blacks. Appleby believed that he himself concealed behind an impenetrable mask his satisfaction in
his son's having thereafter even more surprisingly transformed himself from an Appleby into a Raven. Nearly all
Judith's relations had been – and were – pretty mad. But
they had followed a remarkable variety of curious pursuits. Writing Anglicized versions of the *nouveau roman*
was simply the latest of these. 'Stop bothering about
Bobby,' Appleby shamelessly went on, 'and tell me about
all those Ashmores. I'd like to be clued up on them before
Pride arrives.'

'Very well.' Judith extinguished the small ritual lamp
on her tea-tray. 'The Ashmores have been around these
parts for quite a time. Since the Conquest, in fact.'

'Absolute rubbish. Nobody has been around since the
Conquest – except in the commonplace sense in which we
all have. The Ashmores no doubt emerged from their
hovels in the time of Thomas Cromwell, and liberated
something substantial from a monastery. Not that it's
material. Go on.'

'It certainly wasn't all that number of generations back. Not *their* generations.'

'I know. Their ultimate ancestor was a tortoise. Or a Galapagos turtle. Martyn Ashmore told me all that. His grandmother was present at the Rape of the Lock. I accorded his recital – offered in the presence of appropriate family portraits – instant and implicit belief. But it scarcely appears a factor in the present mystery.'

'I suppose not. But I don't see how I'm going to tell you about the Ashmores if you will go on talking.'

Appleby made a resigned gesture. Then he threw a log on the fire – thereby bringing the looming Hoobin crisis one step nearer – and filled his pipe.

'The Ashmores,' Judith said, 'have a reputation for eccentricity. They've had it for a long time, and occasionally it seems to deepen into madness. That must be the Chief Constable's excuse for ignoring Martyn Ashmore when he started some tale of mysterious persecution over a glass of sherry.'

'Pride didn't exactly ignore it. He had somebody go round asking discreet questions. But nothing emerged. And it seems that Ashmore wasn't in any sense asking for help. It was this neighbour business again – feeling it due to a fellow to tell him about something that was going on. And if that isn't nearer to madness than to eccentricity I don't know what is.'

'If that's one salient point about Martyn Ashmore, another is his wealth. There's far more money than simply comes to him from land.'

'That's not quite what he suggested to me. He implied that it was safe, broad acres with him, and what I remember his calling bubble-and-squeak stock-jobbing in his numerous relations.'

'He was being less than candid.' Judith appeared in no doubt about this. 'It's combining a large fortune with really miserly habits that has given him so picturesque a reputation.'

'There didn't seem to be a servant about the place. He said they demand exorbitant wages.'

'I think he was being less than candid again. There are said to be some old creatures lurking around the place, although he refuses to have them quartered in the house. As to the whole family, I don't know much about them in recent years – not really since they used to be around when I was a girl. Martyn wasn't the head of the family. An elder brother had the Chase, and was married and had a son. Martyn inherited only because his brother and nephew were killed in a motor smash. There were two younger brothers who are still in circulation, although they aren't at all young now. And there are nephews and nieces, and great-nephews and great-nieces. Even the younger ones are much in these parts from time to time. Shall we have a big party and ask the lot? You could go round questioning them closely. That would clue you up.'

'I think not. But I'd like to know more about the French side – for instance how Martyn Ashmore's French ancestry landed him in France, and in what capacity, during the war. That young Frenchman, de Voisin, puzzles me quite a lot. Why on earth should he have turned up like that?'

'Might he have been the villain of the piece? Might it have been he who chucked the stone?'

'In theory, yes – although it would have involved some very funny business with a motor-cycle engine. The only clear point is that his arrival on that particular day cannot conceivably have been purely coincidental.'

'You used to say that the most inconceivable coincidences just do happen.'

'They weren't happening at Ashmore Chase.' Appleby paused to allow for his wife's amusement before this dogmatic statement. 'I'd like to *help* this chap.'

'The mysteriously irruptive Jules de Voisin?'

'Of course not. Ashmore. He's so queerly discontinuous that he's hard to assess. But he's not a bad old chap. Kept some sort of end up under pressure both from within and without. And he has some uncommonly good claret.'

'Obviously a worthy object of benevolence. But do you think –'

'Colonel Pride, my lady,' a voice said at the door.

6

'My dear fellow, I'm most grateful to you.' The Chief Constable turned to Appleby with these words as soon as he had greeted Judith with the familiarity of an old friend. 'I ought to have been more on my toes when old Ashmore first spun me his unlikely yarn. No smoke without fire, and all that. No tea.'

'No tea?' Appleby was perplexed by this expression.

'Talking to your wife, my dear chap. Had tea. Shouldn't be surprised if I'm still here when it's time for a drink though. A good deal to beat out. Plot thickens, as a matter of fact.'

'Toast your toes,' Appleby said hospitably. 'Evenings turning chilly now. You've found some sort of substantiation of Martyn Ashmore's story?'

'Well, yes and no.' Pride turned again to Judith. 'Is this going to bore you, my dear? Your husband's told you about it?'

'He'll talk of nothing else. And you'll remember, Tommy, how reliable I was as a small girl. All those sworn secrets.'

'Yes, of course. That business of Anthea Killcanon's pony, eh? The old pheasant lord was furious.'

'New light on the French yarn?' Appleby prompted. He found a slight tedium in Pride's and Judith's colloquies of this order.

'Yes, decidedly yes. Some of your old henchmen at the Yard doing their stuff splendidly. Been on the line to them on and off all day. Mind you, we must distinguish. No compulsion to believe everything the old fellow says – or even believes. We have just the one hard fact still.'

'It was certainly quite adequately hard.'

'Quite so. It must have been a deuced near thing for both you and Ashmore. And for Ashmore there *have* been other deuced near things. That's what I've turned up. But those really on record happened long ago. And in France. He stuck it out in France, it seems, for some years – in fact until he inherited this place over here. And there *were* attempts on his life – attempts which were undoubtedly a sequel to the grim business he told you about. No question, our people think, of his having played any sort of double game. Perfectly honourable above-board chap, caught up in desperate affairs. But there were plenty of people a bit off their rockers over there in the years after the war. Something had been screwed out of him in a manner unfit to be talked about. Unfortunately there were people who didn't believe in the real existence of – well, the screw. As a consequence, he was shot at, had his house set fire to in the night, and was sent infernal machines inside wine bottles. Common form for a time. Bit of national what's it-called. Psychosis.'

'I was telling Judith as much,' Appleby stirred the logs in the big fireplace. 'But after that?'

'There's the nub of the matter. The business of an annual persecution strikes these back-room types in London as most improbable. Bosh, in fact. They never and nowhere heard of such a thing. And I myself will believe *that* part of the yarn when it too is vouched for by somebody a little more reliable than this old chap seems to be. I've tackled him myself, I may say. But he manages to be uncommonly elusive. At times he seems to imply that these demonstrations, or whatever you'd call them, have been going on ever since he left France. At other times it seems as if only the last few years are in question. For that matter, they're the crucial ones for us. Trail not too cold, eh? Get him to detail some of the alleged circumstances, and we might just conceivably pick up something like corroborative testimony. But I wouldn't put money on it.'

53

'But suppose,' Judith said, 'that Martyn Ashmore is actually killed just short of a year from now. This story that he put on record with you, Tommy, would be the only context, conceivably, available to you in order to make any sense of his death. In fact it would come back to you – and perhaps to others to whom he has told it – in rather a devastating way.'

'In what might be an uncommonly confusing way.' Pride glanced from Judith to Appleby, and hesitated. 'Do you know? I have one damned odd notion in my head. But I rather think I'll keep it under my hat until I've thought over it a bit more. Nothing in it, likely enough.'

'Then I'll be more rash.' Appleby was careful not to appear amused. 'It's just conceivable that the odd notion in your head is an odd notion in my head too. Somebody has it in for Ashmore on grounds which have nothing to do with that ghastly French affair. And that somebody is confusing the old gentleman, and consequently confusing us, by cooking up a spurious connection with it.'

'Just so.' Pride appeared a little crestfallen that he held no monopoly in this idea, but a moment later he chuckled amiably. 'And in that event, I suppose, we should have to estimate the degree of malice intended. You see what I mean? Is it proposed just to give Ashmore a bad time every year? Or are these demonstrations – however many or few there may actually have been – intended to climax in the real thing?'

'It may be,' Judith said, 'that if Mr Ashmore was actually killed – say next year – the intensive investigation you would set going might turn up real evidence of previous attempts, or apparent attempts, and all with something of the Cross of Lorraine association attached to them. And away your people would go, hallooing and baying in that direction. But it would be a false scent, very deliberately contrived.'

'It's a theory that isn't quite plain sailing,' Appleby, having produced this, paused as if to consider his abrupt shift from a hunting to a nautical metaphor. 'We have to take account of the precise character of what occurred the other morning. Of course it's easy a little to misinterpret just what has been happening in the second or two before one has nearly been killed. But I can't believe that the stone came over that parapet blindly. The chap must have been aware of my presence, and presumably of my being a total stranger to him. And he lobbed the thing over, therefore, equally in a hit-or-miss way in relation to either the one or the other of us. Do I make myself clear? It was quite likely that he would kill neither of us – indeed the actual cold probability might be estimated as lying that way. But he very well *might* have killed one of us. He *might* have killed Ashmore – who was clearly the *relevant* one of us in the context of that scratched symbol on the roof – or he *might* have killed me. It's a difficulty that has to be faced in considering any annual-build-up theory.'

'But you have to consider,' Pride said, 'that fellows who go in for that sort of thing often get surprisingly muddled. All calculation one moment, and completely random behaviour the next. Or so I've read in the books on criminology. We don't get much experience of that sort of thing in these parts' – Pride innocently winked at Judith – 'or didn't until your husband came along. Mustn't make a joke, though, of a bad affair like this.'

'What we're considering is that there may be a kind of joke at the heart of it,' Appleby said. 'A thoroughly evil joke. But you're absolutely right about the criminal mind – or rather about any mind wrought to plan and perpetrate something like murder. Calculation and rationality can suddenly go by the board, and something quite unpremeditated, and even quite profitless and meaningless, take their place. That's why detective stories are of no interest to policemen. Their villains remain far too consistently cerebral.'

'*You* wouldn't have remained very cerebral, either – not if that hunk of roof had copped you.' Even before he had concluded this reflection, Colonel Pride looked conscience-stricken. 'Sorry, my dear,' he said to Judith. 'Rotten sort of crack, eh? Fact is – come to feel much at home here.' The Chief Constable, if not embarrassed, was diffident. He turned to Appleby. 'Been on my mind for some time. John and Tommy, perhaps? Seems reasonable sort of thing.'

Appleby gravely agreed to this somewhat heavily promulgated advance in relations. It seemed, moreover, the moment at which to produce the sherry. He had just addressed himself to this task when there was a sudden roar from outside the house. Bobby Appleby had arrived.

It seemed to Judith that the two men might well be left alone, so she followed her common habit when any of the children turned up and went hospitably out into the open air. The autumn dusk had already fallen, and mist was drifting up from the river and curling round the house; out of this Bobby's car seemed to thrust a bonnet of disproportionate size, as in a badly focused photograph. Behind this two bear-like figures were in process of heaving themselves out of the front seats while simultaneously shedding shaggy outer integuments; the car was an open one, and both had been appropriately attired.

'Hullo, Mum!' Bobby called. 'Here we are, unscratched but perished. This is Finn.'

The appearance called Finn – he seemed quite as large as Bobby – advanced amid awkward contortions which stemmed from the difficulty of shaking hands while half-way out of a duffel-coat.

'Oh, I say!' Finn said. 'How do you do? Frightfully kind of you Lady Appleby, to offer to put me up. Bobby's always babbling about Dream. Wanted to see it for ages.'

Lady Appleby – whose practised glance had already penetrated to the back of the car and distinguished not one suitcase but two – made a suitable reply. She couldn't recall that she had ever heard her son speak of a friend called Finn. Perhaps they had been at school together – in which case Finn might be a surname. Or the young man might belong to Bobby's Balliol period – and then he would be Finn plus some further appellation which the elder Applebys might or might not learn before he went away again. It at least seemed unlikely that Finn was part of Bobby's new and literary life. At least he didn't *sound* literary. Perhaps he too had achieved the distinction of a match against the All Blacks.

'Funny that Finn's never been down before,' Bobby said, and tossed the suitcases out of the car as if they had been handbags or school satchels. 'Where shall I put him, Mummy? In the haunted room?'

'Well, it is the haunted room that I've prepared for him.' Having managed this polite prevarication – which she could see that Bobby appreciated – Judith turned to her totally unexpected guest. 'The haunted room is the one with a bathroom,' she explained. 'Most people feel it balances up.'

'Oh, I say! Yes – what fun!' Finn – or Mr Finn – appeared slightly at a loss. He scarcely seemed to be of what could be called an intellectual habit, or likely to be *au fait* with the *nouveau roman* world. Perhaps, for professional purposes and in quest of 'copy', Bobby was reviving an acquaintance with uncomplicated types. 'Jolly good!' Finn said – perhaps a little overdoing things. 'I don't a bit mind a ghost.'

'I'm so glad. But I may just mention that the bathroom is a modern addition, and the ghost never enters it. If the ghost turns tedious, you just go and have another bath.'

'Yes, I see.' Finn sounded puzzled rather than suspicious, so that Judith took an honest vow not to make further fun of him.

'You're in splendid time for dinner,' she said. 'Bobby will steer you round, and bring you down for drinks.'

'Oh, thanks most awfully!' They were now in the hall, which Finn was surveying with large rather than merely civil admiration. 'I say, jolly fine! Marvellous base for operations – eh, Bobby?'

'Yes, of course.' Bobby Appleby appeared to feel – very

properly – that this naïve remark called for explanation. 'As I was saying, Mummy, it's odd Finn's never been to Dream before. He has a lot of friends in these parts, and we're going to look them up. Not close by, actually, but on the other side of the downs. People we haven't met, I think, since we moved into the old home. But you must know all about them. The Ashmores at King's Yatter. And I suppose the other Ashmores – the ones at Abbot's Yatter – as well.'

7

'Finn has rung up one of his pals,' Bobby Appleby announced an hour later. He had come downstairs before his friend, evidently with the very proper aim of putting his parents a little more in the picture. 'Giles.'

'I don't think I know anybody called Giles in these parts,' Appleby said. 'But no doubt your mother does.'

'No, no, Dad. Not Dash Giles Esquire. Giles Ashmore, the son and heir of the King's Yatter lot. Finn and this Giles were after the same girl. Name of Robina.'

'I don't believe it. No girl with a name like Robina could possibly have two suitors simultaneously.'

'Well, this one had – and it seems to be Giles Ashmore who has got away with her. But of course it brought Finn and Giles together.'

'How very odd!' Appleby turned to Judith. 'Competition in that sphere is commonly regarded as divisive, wouldn't you say?'

'Not at all.' Bobby seemed to judge it unnecessary to give his mother time to reply. Although essentially a modest youth, he was inclined to regard himself as the family's authority on human relationships. 'One gets terribly thick with a chap who wants the same girl. As a matter of fact, Finn wants to give this Giles a bit of a leg up. That's partly why he's come down to Dream.'

'I see.' Appleby provided his son with a glass of sherry. 'A leg up with Robina?'

'No, not exactly with Robina. As a matter of fact, Finn seems rather to have stopped talking about her. Giles is in some sort of family scrape or difficulty, and Finn thinks it would be decent to lend a hand.'

'Your father,' Judith said, 'also has benevolent impulses towards an Ashmore. But an older one. By the way, your friend doesn't happen to have invited Mr Giles Ashmore to dinner? I ought perhaps just to know.'

'Of course not!' Bobby appeared decently astonished. 'Only to drive across and drop in afterwards. I suppose all those Ashmores are old family friends.'

'Before the Flood,' Judith said. 'Your great-uncle Everard knew them all. And of course we'll be glad to see the young man. As a matter of fact, I think your father has some notion of extending his acquaintance among the whole Ashmore tribe.'

'Then he can begin with this one.' Bobby glanced curiously at his father; he was a young man whose mind was readily prompted to speculation. 'Wasn't that Colonel Pride who was here when Finn and I arrived?'

'It was Tommy,' Appleby said. 'In future when you meet him you will address him as "Tommy" and not as "Sir". But you will preface this familiarity with a suitably diffident speech. Verbs ought not to figure in it.'

'I'll remember.' Bobby turned to his mother. 'Daddy can't forget, can he, that our excellent Chief Constable was one of your earliest loves? But you'll find it's a basis on which they eventually get tremendously chummy. Like Finn and this Giles because of Robina.'

Appleby's first reaction to Mr Giles Ashmore was one of surprise that he was quite young. This was irrational. It was clear that a contemporary of Bobby's and of the character called Finn *ought* to be quite young. But Appleby had arrived at the persuasion that all Ashmores must be, if not old, at least ageless. As here one may find a bevy of maidens, roes, quails, or larks, or there simply a gaggle of geese so on the farther side of the downs (he had come to suppose) there dwelt a crawl of tortoises, and Ashmore was the name of each.

But Giles Ashmore could be described only as immature,

as having indeed scarcely as yet developed a carapace. Perhaps it was in compensation for this that he appeared to have a somewhat excessive interest in old armour. The late Luke Raven (who, unlike his great-nephew, had been a poet and not an anti-novelist) had during his post-William Morris phase accumulated various chunks of chain-mail, the continued rusting presence of these in various unregarded corners of Dream was the occasion of young Mr Ashmore's embarking on the subject at somewhat tedious length.

He had arrived a shade early for an after-dinner call, and Judith had marked the circumstance by inviting him to wash the sherry glasses. He had taken this outrage – Appleby judged – extremely well; it was undeniable that, even if rather a bore, he had deserved his coffee and brandy when these came along. He was a nervous youth – one felt one knew why the notion of an artificial skin of steel attracted him – and gave the impression of being only imperfectly in contact with material things. If Robina (as Appleby somehow suspected) was very much a material thing, it was hard to imagine how he could have got away with her. One would have supposed that Finn – although he seemed to specialize in being a Bertie Wooster or Bingo Little type – would make the running every time. But Giles no doubt had something which, even with a Robina, counted for something. Perhaps it was just being an Ashmore. Giles, one supposed, had a pretty clear recollection of relatives who had been edified by Joseph Addison or got drunk with Dick Steele. Perhaps Robina was sensitive to things of that sort.

Finn did a good deal of the talking – quite enough to suggest that he was the master mind behind whatever hopeful design was going forward. And certainly there was a design. It wasn't at all possible for the elder Applebys to feel that the charm of their company alone had drawn to Dream these two oddly assorted friends of Bobby's. It was true that Giles Ashmore seemed as ready to stare round about him as to talk – perhaps in the hope of spotting an interesting basinet or placcate from Luke Raven's collection. He did not suggest himself as a very enterprising young man. If he was in a scrape – as Bobby had suggested – he would certainly need friends to haul him out of it.

'You see,' Finn said expansively to Judith, 'old Giles is all fixed up to get married. Jolly good, don't you think?'

Judith agreed that it was jolly good. The reference could only be to Robina, and it could only be presumed that Finn's magnanimity in relation to his and old Giles's late rivalry was unflawed. This seemed probable enough; nothing in Finn suggested what could be called a brooding temperament.

'But there's trouble about the mun,' Finn went on. 'Giles hasn't any, and he hasn't even a fat pay-packet to look forward to later on. That's right, Giles?'

'That's right.' Giles's reply was absent – perhaps because he had just spotted the gorget by Jacob Topf which had been the most notable of Luke's acquisitions.

'You see, he wants to curate things in a museum,' Finn went on, 'and it isn't a career that leaves you rolling. But the real trouble is that Giles's father is feeling the wind a bit.'

'I see,' Judith said, and for a moment cast around for a diversion. It didn't seem proper that the *res angusta domi* at King's Yatter should be familiarly canvassed to virtual strangers in this way. But then she remembered that John was becoming curious about the whole tribe of Ashmores, and she let Finn go on.

'Things not too good in the City,' Finn amplified. 'That kind of thing. So Giles's father feels that, if Giles wants *both* to marry *and* to curate he ought to have found somebody well in the mun herself. But, of course, love isn't like that at all. It isn't this girl's fault that she hasn't got a bean.'

'But perhaps,' Appleby asked helpfully, 'she has at least some means of honest earning?'

'Well, yes – she has. Just at the moment she has. She sings, as a matter of fact. A bit of dancing too. At a place in London. You wouldn't know it.'

'Probably not. So Giles's present predicament is essentially economic?'

'That's it!' Finn seemed to feel that Appleby had penetrated to the heart of an intricate mystery. 'And that's where Giles's uncle – or perhaps it's his great-uncle – comes in.'

'Martyn Ashmore?'

'Jolly good, sir.' Finn's manner positively suggested a small round of applause. 'That's where the family mun is. Giles, that's right?'

Giles Ashmore nodded. He was attending now, but with an appearance of some gloom.

'So something has to be done. Giles has to bestir himself. Think of all those generations of enterprising Ashmores. That sort of thing.'

'Armour rusting on the walls,' Bobby Appleby interposed, 'on the blood of Clifford calls. Seize the lance. Bear me to the heart of France. That right, Giles?'

Giles Ashmore – whom it appeared customary to attempt to rouse by means of this formula – smiled wanly, and then ventured to speak.

'Well, yes,' he said. 'Must do something. And Uncle Martyn seems the man.'

'Only there's been a coolness,' Finn said. 'Bit of bad blood, and all that. Happens in families, wouldn't you say? Happened in yours, I expect, Lady Appleby.'

'Uncle Martyn might weigh in with something handsome?' Appleby asked – rather hastily, since he felt Judith might not reply wholly urbanely to Finn's last speculation. He was himself beginning to feel Bobby's friends to be tiresome. Young men forming improbable plans to 'touch' a rich relative struck him as a somewhat faded species of comedy. He wondered why Bobby was mixed up in it. Perhaps there lurked in it something more interesting than at present appeared. 'It is even perhaps relevant,' he added, 'that this wealthy kinsman has no obvious heir?'

'All that sort of thing.' Giles Ashmore nodded without much conviction. 'Finn says that even if he carved up quite handsomely among the whole crowd of us, it mightn't be for a dishearteningly long time. I don't know whether you happen to be aware of it, sir, but the Ashmores are an exceptionally long-lived lot.'

'It is, as a matter of fact, information that has lately come my way.' Giles, Appleby was thinking, if not eager was at least candid. 'It would appear that what you have in mind is a gift rather than a bequest?'

'Well, yes. For a start, anyway.'

There was a moment's silence. Appleby was aware of Judith as refraining from looking at the clock. Young Mr Ashmore's mercenary designs would be less depressing, she was probably feeling, if advanced with rather more *élan*. This seemed also to be Finn's view, for he now intervened again on a livelier note.

'So the question,' he said, 'is ways and means. Good phrase, don't you think? My father's an M.P., and he's on something called the Committee of Ways and Means. Does all the thinking up of how to raise the wind. We're a committee like that now.'

'You must not regard my wife and myself as having been co-opted,' Appleby said. 'And perhaps your deliberations ought to be in private.'

'Oh, we're not thinking of anything underhand!' There was an offended note in Finn's voice. 'We just have to find the sound psychological approach. Make sure we know the sort of old boy we're dealing with. Bobby says he's a pathological miser, like somebody in Proust.'

'Balzac,' Bobby said.

'It's the same idea. Would you say, sir, that Bobby's right?'

'Certainly not. My acquaintance with Mr Martyn Ashmore is both recent and slight. But I'm not in a position to say that Bobby is *wrong*. And if you have estimated Mr

Ashmore's disposition accurately, he would appear to be a particularly unpromising person to whom to direct an application of the kind envisaged – would he not?' Appleby frowned as he spoke. He was never pleased when he heard himself producing this kind of sub-ironic note. 'And I'm blessed if I'd know how to begin, anyway.'

'Genuine cheer,' Finn said readily. 'We think he probably feels lonely, and only imagines he dislikes his relations as he seems to say he does. Waiting to be approached, really. If he can just be given the impression that Giles is really fond of him –'

'But is Giles really fond of him? I seem to have gathered that he knows virtually nothing about him.'

'Then he will thaw at once,' Finn concluded, unheeding. 'There will be a benefit all round.'

'Because old Mr Ashmore,' Bobby amplified with every appearance of gravity, 'will be drawn back into the main stream of wholesome family affections and solicitudes, and Giles will be given the means of uniting himself to his Robina forthwith. Giles, isn't that –'

'Yes, that's right,' Giles Ashmore said automatically.

The fire was burning low. Appleby, obeying the iron law of hospitality, put another log on it, and thought gloomily of Hoobin and Hoobin's birthday whisky. This at least diverted his mind from the childish confabulation going forward. It was his wife's name that recalled him to it.

'And it's about this,' Finn was saying, 'that we want Lady Appleby's advice. It seems clear to us that Giles should simply drive up to the front door of the Chase – or better perhaps walk up – and ring the bell.'

'Excellent,' Appleby said. 'Only I'm inclined to think that he ought first to take out a life assurance policy. Made in the lady's favour. But go on.'

'I suppose he ought to think of that sort of thing.' Not unnaturally, Finn was a little at a loss. 'Giles should simply pay a friendly family call. Only we feel that he ought to take a present to the old boy. Something really appealing and likely to soften the heart. What do you think, Lady Appleby? What would you advise? Remember he's a shocking old miser – or so they say – who lives more or less on dog-biscuits and water. Would a Stilton be a good idea?'

'I doubt whether Stilton is the right cheese with dog-biscuits. And if Mr Ashmore is really penurious he will only use it to bait his mouse-traps.' Judith paused as if in serious thought. 'I'd be inclined to advise something mice don't care for.'

'Or bats or owls,' Bobby said. 'Ashmore Chase is quite certain to abound in them.'

'I know!' Giles suddenly said. It was his first moment of perceptible animation, so that everybody stared at him. 'A bottle of wine.'

'Or a dozen bottles of wine.' The expansive nature of Finn was at play here. 'More than that might be awkward. Kind of Father Christmas effect. But a case would be just the thing.'

'You mean I'd have to walk up the drive with it?' Giles asked apprehensively. 'Wouldn't it be a bit heavy?'

'Perhaps, in that case, you could drive, after all. I think it's just the thing. A gentleman can always drop in on another gentleman with a dozen bottles of wine. It's always happening to my father.' Finn looked gratefully at Judith. 'A first-rate notion. We'll get hold of the stuff in the morning.'

'I think –' Appleby began – and then checked himself and said something else. Why should he say disillusioning things about Château Lafite to these cheerful young idiots? 'I think,' he said gravely, 'that you will find a reputable licensed grocer next door to the post-office in Linger.'

'Then that's fine!' A blessed moment had come, for Finn was on his feet – and plainly with the intention of shoving Giles Ashmore out of the house. 'We'll collect the stuff in the morning, and push the whole thing through. Giles, that's right?'

Perhaps because he was advancing politely upon Lady Appleby, Giles Ashmore for a moment made no reply. But when he spoke, it was with surprising decision.

'The whole thing,' he said. 'We'll push it through.'

8

Appleby's interest in the numerous Ashmores of King's Yatter, Abbot's Yatter, and other rural localities on the farther side of the downs was surprisingly gratified on the following day. Armed with a chain-saw, he had spent a good part of the morning coping with the impending timber crisis. On the ground was an aged and twisted oak, brought down by the October gales. Standing by – also aged and twisted, but as yet resistant to the seasons – was Hoobin, equipped with an axe and a wheelbarrow. Appleby's task was to saw the trunk and larger branches into sections, shear away the smaller branches, and pause every now and then to take up a second axe and help his assistant to catch up with the cleaving. Every now and then, also, Hoobin would load the barrow with the logs and amble off to the wood-shed. It was on his return from one of these missions that he paused, eyed with critical appraisal his employer's manipulation of the chain-saw, and then drew from a pocket an enormous silver watch.

'Gone eleven,' Hoobin said above the uproar of the saw.

'What of it?' It had to be admitted that Hoobin's age asked ease, and in this interest he had in fact spent a placid quarter of an hour with a pipe some time after ten o'clock.

'Doctor Verity do go out on his rounds come eleven.' Hoobin spoke with gloomy satisfaction. 'And there be times when only haste will serve.'

'No doubt.' With what he was conscious of as foolish bravado, Appleby performed an intricate manoeuvre with the chain-saw. It was an implement the lethal potentialities of which it would be rash to question. But that Hoobin should be rapt in a gratifying inward vision of an amputated and writhing employer was faintly disagreeable even to one well-acquainted with the harmless vagaries of the rustic mind. So Appleby attempted distraction. 'Hoobin,' he asked, 'have you any acquaintance over at the Yatters?'

Hoobin put down his axe. Although not to be described as of a conversible habit, he was not averse to talk when he judged it not compatible with labour.

'My brother Alfred,' Hoobin said, 'has worked for Farmer Blowbody – at Low Yatter, that be – these forty year. And these forty year have I heard never a report on him.'

'You've heard nothing of a brother in a neighbouring parish, as it almost is, for forty years?'

Some slight note of surprise in Appleby's voice perhaps offended Hoobin, for he remained broodingly silent (without however taking up his axe) for a full minute. And then he spoke.

'Words passed,' Hoobin said.

'I'm very sorry to hear it. Is Alfred married, and with a family? It seems a pity you shouldn't make it up.'

Hoobin was again silent for a space – plainly to mark his scorn of this flaccid suggestion. He then condescended to take up the question that had preceded it.

'A wife there be, and childer too. But none come my way. Or none but Solo – and that only because I be a perusing man.'

It was undeniable that Hoobin was a perusing man. He owned a pair of spectacles which proved the point, and was even rumoured to be a subscriber to the local weekly paper. Indeed it was this paper which proved to be in question now. Solo Hoobin – he was apparently among the younger of Alfred Hoobin's numerous progeny – had lately figured in this public print. This had been because of the assault committed upon him by Mr Ambrose Ashmore of Abbot's Yatter. Appleby's Hoobin, although of late so sadly estranged from his kinsfolk, must have followed this large rural scandal closely, for he was able to give a surprisingly particular account of it.

Solo, it appeared, had been employed by Mr Ambrose Ashmore in the humble but honourable condition of a garden boy, and he had come to regard a certain toll or levy upon his employer's orchard as a legitimate perquisite. As a consequence of this, Mr Ashmore had one day come upon him with his pockets full of Worcester Pearmains. Whereupon (according to Solo) Mr Ashmore had surprisingly produced an enormous whip and belaboured Solo with it to such good – or ill – effect that Solo's parents had been constrained to take the boy to the doctor. Eventually the matter had come before the gentry on their Bench ('All magistrates be gentry,' Hoobin had explained). And the magistrates had brought it out that Mr Ambrose Ashmore had acted only in the most playful – not to say affectionate – manner, and that Solo's injuries were the consequence of his father's subsequent stern view of his delinquency. In other words, according to the official view of the matter, Mr Ambrose Ashmore had unlawfully but venially flicked at Solo's shoulders with a switch; Solo's father had larruped him; and Solo's mother had – unnecessarily but again venially – called in medical aid. The summons against Mr Ashmore had been dismissed on the ground that the magistrates didn't want to be bothered with it. (Their clerk, Appleby imagined, had been able to remind them that *de minimis non curat lex*.) Solo's father had been rebuked. And Solo himself had promptly been given employment by Mr Rupert Ashmore of King's Yatter – a gentleman who appeared to be on as bad terms (or at least non-terms) with his brother Ambrose as was Appleby's Hoobin with his brother Alfred. But brothers be often that way inclined, Hoobin pointed out. For blood be thicker than water, after all.

Appleby, after allowing himself to be for a moment diverted by this monstrous perversion of an edifying and ancient saw, thought to inquire of Hoobin whether he had any further information about Mr Ambrose Ashmore. Hoobin had. What had made the discomfiting experience of young Solo really awkward for Mr Ashmore and his honest supporters on the Bench was the well-known fact that Mr Ashmore had proved a man of somewhat violent temper on certain other and totally different occasions. As a younger man – much younger, it was true – he had stripped naked and then vigorously cleansed under a fire-hose a neighbouring gentleman who had chanced to offend him. This had taken place in the presence of ladies and at a hunt ball. Such conduct, it was generally felt, would have been appropriate and agreeable only at a farmers' dinner. On another occasion it appeared that Mrs Ambrose Ashmore had outlandishly employed a cook of the male sex, and her husband had wasted little time before picking up this unnatural creature and pitching him through a window and into a flower-bed. Unfortunately the man had very cleverly contrived to break an arm as he fell, so there had been a good deal of fuss and a substantial bill for damages. The bill was no doubt the more awkward in that Mr Ambrose Ashmore was understood to be in circumstances so reduced that his wife, far from hiring a Frenchman with an absurd high hat, ought to have been at the kitchen range herself.

All this – if not in precisely such words – Appleby extracted from Hoobin between one bout of chain-sawing and the next. Hoobin also proved to have what might be termed genealogical interests. Rupert Ashmore of King's Yatter was an elder brother of the violent Ambrose Ashmore of Abbot's Yatter, and both were the juniors of the great Squire Martyn Ashmore of Ashmore Chase, a person of fabulous wealth whose grandfather had been one of the great men of the land in the famous times of Oliver Cromwell.

It appeared – Appleby thought – that the tortoise-aspect of the Ashmores had bred quite a lively mythology of its own. And Rupert Ashmore, who had pleasantly expressed his attitude to his brother Ambrose by taking the savagely fustigated Solo Hoobin into his employment, was of course the father of Giles Ashmore, Appleby's young guest of the evening before. And Giles's father too had been reported as impoverished. Perhaps both younger brothers urgently required that the miserly Martyn should mount a rescue operation.

These reflections lasted Appleby through one of Hoobin's leisured disappearances round the corner of the house with his barrow. His return, this time, was at a perceptibly quickened pace. This could only mean that he had displeasing intelligence to communicate. And so it proved. With a jerk of his thumb down the garden path he indicated that his employer had a duty to perform.

'Company,' Hoobin said with relish.

Judith had received two visitors in the drawing-room and was engaging them in civil conversation. But plainly she was only holding the fort, and their concern was with her husband. The first was young and the second elderly. The first Appleby recognized with some surprise at once; it was Jules de Voisin. The second had a vaguely familiar air, and he seemed to be claiming some uncertain sort of acquaintanceship with Judith. It came to Appleby suddenly that here was one of Martyn Ashmore's brothers. And in this he proved to be right. It was Rupert Ashmore, father of the unimpressive Giles, who was paying this mysterious call.

De Voisin's bearing was alert, watchful, and stiffly formal, so that one might have supposed something hostile about him. But Appleby felt that this would not be quite accurate; it was rather as if the young man was finding himself progressively involved in a situation which was far from agreeable to him. Rupert Ashmore, on the other hand, softly radiated a sympathetic manner. He might have arrived on some visit of condolence as such things were conducted in the Victorian era. But as the Applebys had not been bereaved this surely seemed inapposite, and it indeed presently transpired that Rupert Ashmore's condolences were being offered to the universe at large. The universe was in the habit of behaving very badly, he seemed to say – as for example when it shoved forward into the regard of his son Giles a young woman so deplorably ineligible as the musical but impecunious Robina. Nevertheless the universe probably felt properly apologetic about such tiresome performances, so that it was impossible not to feel sorry for it.

Not that Mr Rupert Ashmore had anything to say about his son. He appeared unaware of Giles's visit to the Applebys on the previous evening, and his concern was with his brother Martyn. It was very much a concern. His brother Martyn was worrying him greatly. This was the occasion of his venturing to introduce himself to Sir John.

'But I think,' Appleby said mildly, 'that you may have mistaken my degree of familiarity with your brother. I have been to the Chase only once – as a trespasser, as a matter of fact, and only a couple of days ago. It is true that your brother was kind enough to entertain me to a most agreeable luncheon. And the same occasion gave me the happiness of making the acquaintance of Monsieur de Voisin.' Appleby looked solemnly at Judith as he produced these well rounded phrases. He was defying her, more or less, to be improperly amused by them. 'So I feel hardly qualified to assist you in any intimate family matter. Or perhaps I am mistaken? It certainly seems to me that it is something of the sort that is on your mind.'

'But indeed it is!' Mr Rupert Ashmore gave to this admission an air of handsome acknowledgement. 'And of course neither Jules nor I would have dreamed of disturbing you, my dear Sir John, had you not been involved at the Chase – as Jules has informed me – in an unfortunate incident which you were so very kind as to pass over in your mention a few moments ago of meeting my brother Martyn the other day. After that meeting, I can hardly hope to suppose that the truth about Martyn is unknown to you. He is deranged – mentally deranged.' Mr Rupert

Ashmore made a helpless gesture. 'It is, alas, an affliction of long standing. My brother did not have a very good war.'

'That painful period,' Jules de Voisin suddenly struck in in his impeccable English, 'has left him a legacy of systematized delusions. It was in an endeavour to persuade him of their total lack of substance that I visited him the other day. Certain persuasions in which he has indulged have occasioned considerable distress to his relations in France. But I have myself a further reason to feel much concerned. I have the honour to be betrothed to Virginia, Mr Rupert Ashmore's daughter.'

'I see.' Appleby looked candidly at the young Frenchman. 'That certainly gives you more than a footing with any Ashmores who may be around. But I'm not quite clear how I myself can be of help to you – any more than to Mr Ashmore here, either. Would one of you perhaps explain?'

'Mr Rupert Ashmore would like to have your sense – do I express myself correctly? – of what happened the other day. You will recall that I was not myself an actual witness of the incident. But it would appear that Mr Martyn Ashmore exercised a quite diabolical degree of ingenuity on this occasion.'

'Ingenuity, Monsieur de Voisin? I can't think what you are talking about.'

'Let me interrupt.' Rupert Ashmore had leant politely forward, offering a soothing gesture the while to the world at large. 'My brother's delusions – the belief that he is pursued by emissaries of some French underground organization which he offended long ago – inevitably attract less and less credence as the years pass. So this year there has been a fresh development. He actually contrived the appearance of a lethal attack in the presence of a witness. That witness, Sir John, was of course yourself. I am only anxious that you should realize what must have happened.'

'I think I realize very well what must have happened.'

'I feel greatly relieved to hear you say so. It would cloud the issue were we to begin supposing that Martyn's life is actually in any danger.'

'The issue is certainly sufficiently clouded already.' Appleby was beginning to find this a very odd conversation indeed. 'But, come to think of it, what, Mr Ashmore, precisely *is* the issue? Just what has to be decided?'

'There can surely be no two answers to that.' Mr Rupert Ashmore permitted himself a momentary expression of civil surprise. 'It is a question of the kindest way to deal with my brother in his dreadful aberration.'

'You mean the most respectable way to get him locked up?'

Mr Rupert Ashmore frowned. He was offended. Perhaps it was fortunate, Appleby reflected, that he was not Mr Ambrose Ashmore, who was on record as given to rash and sudden physical assault. But de Voisin struck smoothly in.

'It is a matter of the stone,' he said. 'The suggestion is that it was dropped, or hurled, by someone lurking above the front door and concealed behind the parapet. But this of course is fantastic, as we are happily agreed.' De Voisin paused for a moment, whether in obscure irony or evidently in the hope of securing Appleby's assent. 'After much thought, we have come to the conclusion that the front door itself is the key to the mystery. Or perhaps *its* key is the key.' De Voisin paused again on this happy turn of phrase. 'Would we be correct in supposing, Sir John, that Mr Ashmore unlocked and threw open his front door, and that it was in this very instant that the thing happened?'

'I am not sure that there was not a sufficient interval for Mr Ashmore to utter a word or two. But your line of thought, Monsieur de Voisin, interests me very much.'

'The stone had been delicately balanced on the parapet. The door beneath, when vigorously thrust open, produced sufficient reverberation to bring it down.'

'I see. But do you acknowledge that, upon this interpretation, your unfortunate English kinsman's madness must extend to a perfect willingness to risk killing himself – or to risk killing a perfect stranger whom he couldn't so much as have counted upon meeting at all?'

'The matter has its perplexities, no doubt. Allow me to say that I am merely putting Mr Rupert Ashmore's point of view.' As he curiously shifted ground in this way, de Voisin favoured his fellow-caller with a formal bow. 'My own concern has merely been to try to disabuse Mr Martyn Ashmore of the nonsensical notion he harbours – or appears to harbour.' De Voisin made one of his pauses on this. 'I owe him that duty, even as the most distant relative. Moreover his fantasies – whether they are pure fantasies or fantastically erroneous explanations of events actually occurring – are a reflection upon the humanity and good sense of my countrymen.'

'And now we must not detain you further.' Rupert Ashmore had stood up. He appeared not too pleased with his French relative. 'My dear Lady Appleby' – he had turned rather elaborately to Judith – 'you will understand that the essential occasion of my call has been to apologize to your husband and yourself for the horrid occurrence at the Chase. And to express the hope that you will find it possible to let the matter rest. You may be assured that we shall all – our whole family, that is to say – deal tactfully but adequately with the consequences of my poor brother's condition. It has been pleasant to meet again after so many years. I am glad that even this shocking business – my dear Appleby, if I may so address you – has enabled me to make your acquaintance.'

With this, Mr Rupert Ashmore fell to shaking hands, and Monsieur de Voisin to making precisely calculated bows. Within a couple of minutes, the visitors had gone.

'Well, I'm blessed.' Appleby, returning from the hall, sank into a chair. 'What on earth was all that in aid of?'

'Discreet exploration, I'd say. They wanted to discover just how hard you were taking the fact of nearly having had your brains dashed out. And what move, if any, you were making about it.'

'Rupert is out to impugn his brother Martyn's sanity. Is the Frenchman regretting having got engaged to the daughter of such a disgusting specimen? He didn't seem to know quite what attitude to take to the whole thing. But he genuinely believes, surely, that the notion of murderous emissaries from across the English Channel is nonsense.'

'I think he does.'

'As for Rupert, I had an odd feeling that he was conscious of having made some utterly false move, and is wondering how to retrieve it. Is there any sense in that?' Appleby looked at the clock. 'Almost lunch time. No point in going out again to urge Hoobin on. Just ten minutes to have a look at *The Times*.' He reached for the paper. 'By the way, what has happened to those young men?'

'Bobby and Finn? They've gone off to join Giles Ashmore again. They said they were going to be out to lunch and dinner, and back late. I expect they're putting their precious plan into operation.'

'They're welcome to it. Only I can't think what Bobby wants with such nonsense.'

'It's just that he's interested in people.'

'I suppose so.' Appleby's tone was already absent; he had opened the paper, and was applying himself to the court page. 'Odd mistake,' he said presently.

'In *The Times*?'

'Yes. Ashmores again. And muddled. Giles's engagement to the beautiful Robina. They've got the family names muddled. They've printed –' He broke off. 'Well, I'm damned! Nothing of the sort.'

'John, what on earth are you talking about?'

'It's not Giles. And not a mistake. I apologize to Printing House Square. Read that.' He handed the paper to Judith. She read in silence the paragraph to which he had pointed.

Forthcoming marriages

Mr Martyn Ashmore and Miss Robina Bunker

The engagement is announced between Martyn Ashmore, eldest surviving son of the late Colonel Ayden Ashmore and of the late Mrs Ashmore (*née* Haut-Bages-Montpelou), of Ashmore Chase, and Robina, daughter of Mr and Mrs Bunker of 'Golf View', Pudsey, Yorkshire.

'How odd,' Judith said, 'if you have a name like Bunker to call your house "Golf View".'

'Perhaps so.' Appleby indicated that he didn't think highly of the relevance of this comment. 'Possibly it's a misprint for "Gulf".'

'I doubt whether there's any gulf at Pudsey.'

'There's no doubt one between rich and poor, and these Bunkers live on one side or the other.'

'We're talking nonsense because *this* is nonsense.' Judith put down *The Times*. 'It doesn't make sense.'

'Not at all. It makes perfect sense. Ashmores have rather a habit of marrying a shade late in life. As a matter of fact, I had the cheek to ask Martyn whether he mightn't have something of the sort in mind himself. And I'm not sure he didn't receive the suggestion with a kind of malign glee. But it's uncommonly odd that he should have pinched Giles's girl.'

'And Finn's girl too, don't forget. He and Giles considered themselves rivals for Robina Bunker's hand. She must be a very efficient little gold-digger. And there's another thing about Giles and Finn. Think of them last night – and Bobby too. The precious trio hadn't a clue about this. I wonder whether they've seen the newspaper today.'

'Probably not.' Appleby chuckled. 'They're possibly fondly engaged in buying that claret from the grocer now.' His expression changed. 'But there's another thing, and it introduces a new dimension into the whole affair. Ashmores don't merely marry at an enormous age. They have a capacity – enviable, no doubt – for begetting children at an enormous age too.'

Part Three

Death at Ashmore Chase

9

Finn had been glancing at a newspaper. He dropped it casually behind the sofa on which he was sprawling as Bobby Appleby entered the bar.

'Hullo, again,' he said cheerfully. 'But where's our helpful friend? He'll be late for opening time.' Finn gestured at the metal grille which still shut off the business end of the room in which they were foregathering. 'Not like Giles. He's one of your six o'clock men.'

'A bit of a drunk?' Bobby asked. He didn't feel that he had as yet got to know Giles Ashmore very well.

'So so. Perhaps he's having a quick one elsewhere, before mucking in with his pals.'

'I hope not. He'll need all his wits, it seems to me, if he's really going to bring off this nonsense of ingratiating himself with his rich uncle. It sounds just not on to me.'

'You ought to know, Bobby.' Finn sounded quite dashed on behalf of their missing companion. 'Writing all that stuff must keep you clued up on how chaps tick.'

'As a matter of fact, I gather Giles has merely gone hunting for his own particular brand of fags. He'll join us here, and we'll have dinner. But I doubt whether it's a good idea.'

'Dinner isn't?' Finn asked. 'I'd usually call it the best idea of the day.'

'This particular dinner, you idiot. Having it before paying the visit of reconciliation, or whatever, to the rich uncle. The old creature lives more or less alone, it seems. Three great oafs piling in on him in darkness may just scare him. Or at least he'll find it very surprising.'

'Good Lord, Bobby, we shan't all three pile in! You

and I will just give Giles a hand to the front door with his precious claret, and then melt into darkness. As for a surprise, it may be Giles who meets with that.'

'What do you mean?'

'Oh, nothing much.' Finn laughed abruptly, and then shook his head. 'This Martyn Ashmore type just mayn't want a virtually unknown nephew turning up with a Father Christmas act. He may simply turf Giles out.'

'Nothing would surprise me less. But if you think so, I don't see why you should encourage Giles in his ploy. He's your pal, not mine.'

'True enough. But it's worth trying. Can't do any harm, you know. Here's the girl who's going to open the bar. What's yours?'

'Tomato juice.'

'Christ!'

'If I'm going to do all the driving on this silly jaunt, Finn, and have a convivial feed beforehand, I'm not going to begin on Martinis. But that needn't inhibit you – or this Giles when he turns up.'

'You are your father's son, Bobby, my boy. That's what *you* are.' Finn lounged to his feet, and suddenly appeared to feel that this had been an improper quip. 'Sorry, man,' he said. 'No offence. I liked your old dad very much. Mum too. I'll pay.' He went over to the bar, and returned with drinks. 'But – do you know? – I thought they'd be better up in all those Ashmores.'

'My mother knows about them, although not in a very up-to-date way. My father's like me, a kind of newcomer in these parts. And I don't know that he very much digs local society. Hasn't this friend-of-your-bosom Giles told you a lot about his relations?'

'He isn't quite that, man. In fact, I didn't know him until we were both after Robina.'

'My parents – since you mention them – think it peculiar that bitter sexual rivalry, and all that, should have brought you and Giles together like Two Musketeers.'

'I expect they think it odd, Bobby, that you make a Third.'

'I expect they do. But they know I'm interested in drop-outs and queer fish. It's my job.'

'Thanks a lot.' Finn raised his glass in unflawed cordiality. 'But you can't call a type who wants to curate things a drop-out. It's a frightfully respectable life. Only, it seems, just no mun.'

'And hence this idiotic expedition. I wish Giles would hurry up with his fags. I'm hungry. But about the Ashmores. There's this aged and well-heeled one at the Chase. Martyn, that is. And Martyn has a brother called Rupert, who is your pal's father –'

'That's right. And Giles, for what it's worth, has a sister, it seems. Name of Virginia, and engaged to some impecunious French relation. Hard cheese on Rupert, wouldn't you say? Two marriages in the offing, and not a bean in either of them.'

'If Rupert is broke, it does, no doubt, have its annoying side. There's another brother, called Ambrose – and I expect he's broke too. And they're all on bad terms with each other. What I haven't gathered, is just the degree of badness. Do they ever as much as see one another? I just haven't any line on that.'

'You must ask Giles.' Finn had finished his Martini, and was looking wistfully at the bar. 'About dinner,' he said. 'I've always thought three a bit awkward. One bottle of wine doesn't really do, and if you have two you feel a bit guilty about going on to brandy and what-not afterwards. Only, of course, if you have things to do afterwards. Like us tonight. You know what I mean? But perhaps, with the car and all, you won't be drinking very much.'

'My full share of that one bottle.' Bobby announced this with proper firmness. 'And here's your fellow-toper turned up at last. Shove some hard liquor down him quick, for the love of mike. I'm starving.'

'Why haven't we got Robina with us?' Finn asked an hour later. There had been two bottles of wine, after all, which had meant five glasses each for Finn and Giles. Finn, in consequence, had become even more cheerful than usual, which was proper enough. Giles appeared unaffected until you noticed the particular way in which his complexion had changed. Bobby concluded that he must add the unknown Giles to the intimately known Finn as not having too good a head. 'Why haven't we got Robina?' Finn repeated to Giles. 'You could present her to the rich uncle.'

'What do you mean – present her?' Giles put down his glass and stared at Finn. He spoke quite loudly, so that in the small hotel dining-room several people turned to glance curiously at the three young men.

'Well, a sort of *droit de seigneur*.' It was clear that this offensive joke wasn't what Finn had intended; it had just come into his head. 'Tied up in pink ribbon. Your uncle might like her quite a lot more than that grocer's claret.'

'Shut up, Finn,' Bobby said.

'No – but honestly. It might be a good idea for Giles to turn up with his girl. Appealing, mightn't it be?' Finn produced an oddly wild laugh. 'At least it would give old Uncle Martyn a surprise.'

'Uncle Martyn has met her, as a matter of fact.' Giles had lowered his voice again, apparently mollified. 'I brought her down to stay, you know, and my parents were quite civilized at first.'

'Before they tumbled to the complete absence of cash?' Finn asked.

'Just that. My mother even toted her around, and included a call at the Chase. My mother tries to keep us on some sort of speaking terms with the head of the family. It isn't much good, but she does go over once or twice a year. Well, Uncle Martyn was very decent to Robina. It seems he saw that she'd had about enough of my mother for a time, and he carried her off for a tour of the house all by herself.' Giles paused before another yelp of laughter from Finn. 'What are you cackling at? Rather hopeful, it seems to me. Would you say it was about time to get cracking?'

'Decidedly it is.' Bobby had glanced at his watch. 'But you'd better not spend more than half an hour with the old gentleman when you get there. He might find anything beyond that a bit boring.'

'Yes, of course,' Giles said readily. He seemed to have formed a high opinion of the sagacity of Finn's literary friend.

'And you must be quite frank about the wine.'

'You mean about its not being all that classy?'

'Partly that. But chiefly you want to appear quite touchingly naïve about this business of bringing him a present. He'll see at once that you want to get something out of him. Be childishly transparent about it. You should find it quite easy.'

'I suppose so.' This time, Giles sounded a little dubious. 'You really think that would be the thing?'

'Definitely. You must amuse him.'

'Tell him jokes?'

'I don't mean that at all. You don't want to put on your clown's hat and start turning somersaults. What you must do is wait till you see that he is finding you an unconsciously absurd young man –'

'His finding that out mayn't show,' Finn interrupted gravely. 'I expect the old boy has quite decent manners.'

'It will be in the air,' Bobby said. 'Giles must wait for it, and then he must suddenly give the game away. Tumble out what he's really after, I mean, and pretty well ask the old gentleman for a cheque there and then – to be followed by a modest transfer of a few useful investments.'

'Shock tactics,' Giles said gravely, and drained his glass with deliberation. 'I don't see why not.'

A sliver of moon hung in a clear sky, but nevertheless it was quite dark in the hotel yard. Finn, climbing into the back of Bobby's car, cursed as the crate of wine dug him in the ribs. He gave it a shove, and then – entirely cheerfully – cursed again.

'The ruddy thing must weigh a ton,' he said. 'Is it really just a dozen of claret?'

'Well, no.' Giles Ashmore, wrapping himself in an aged college scarf, spoke rather reluctantly. 'As a matter of fact, I had the chap put half a dozen bottles of champagne in the bottom. I rather forgot how heavy they are. It's because of the very thick glass.' He turned to Bobby, who had found it necessary to get his head under the bonnet of the Mercedes. 'Do you think that's all right?'

'It sounds to have become rather a massive investment to me. If it's no go, man, you'll have been put back twenty quid, and nothing to show for it. More, if the champagne is drinkable.'

'I don't suppose it's *very* drinkable.' Giles was rather dashed. 'Non-vintage – the stuff you get at weddings and garden-parties.'

'Always drunk it with satisfaction myself,' Finn said. 'And the old don't notice these shades, anyway. Sans teeth, sans eyes, sans taste, you know.'

'And sans everything,' Bobby added. 'I always thought that must be the worst – being sans everything. Just think of it.'

'Yes, of course.' Giles sounded a little vague before this philosophical proposition. He watched Bobby bang down the bonnet and straighten up. 'I say, Bobby, do you know the way?'

'I expect so. Yell out, if you think we're going wrong.' Bobby took his place at the wheel. 'Wind makes a bit of a row, you know. And I'll be opening up, when we get on the downs. Claret, champagne and all, you'll be with Uncle Martyn in a jiffy.'

If this confident prediction did not entirely fulfil itself, it was Bobby Appleby's own fault. They were off on a futile and absurd trip – he told himself as he drove out of the yard – but one wouldn't in so many words say so.

What one would feed through one's typewriter would be not the object in view, or even the thoughts and feelings of his two companions and himself. Only what was tangible and visible must be treated as relevant. And perhaps what one could smell as well. The Mercedes, being ancient, did produce occasional wafts of hot oil, and sometimes one caught a whiff of well-worn leather upholstery too. He liked these smells, and thought they could probably be given a job to do. But the main thing was the movement of the wheel which set a faint light from the instrument panel caressing its two spokes; this, and the quivering needles, and the perplexing flicker near the accelerator which was in fact moonlight coming in over his left shoulder, and his own two knees and his gloved hands: these were the immediate materials for making actual the microcosmic life of the travelling car. And then there was what lay out there in the void, flowing past and protean as it flowed, as it slipped from low moonlight into the glare of his headlamps and out again...

Professional reflections of this *nouvelle écriture* kind caused Bobby to miss a signpost – a fact which Giles Ashmore, who ought to have been alert in the matter, tumbled to only a couple of miles later. The mistake made Bobby impatient, and impatience resulted in his presently overshooting the drive to Ashmore Chase as well. But the mild accident which then followed was not his fault at all. Swinging round a bend at an entirely appropriate speed, he became aware of the headlights of an approaching car. He slackened his pace further, and drew into his proper side of the road. Whereupon the other car, which should similarly have moved in towards its left, moved out towards its right instead. Bobby had just time to say to himself 'yellow lights – French car – forgotten how we drive' when there came a jolt and a nasty sound of crumpling metal. Both cars were at a halt.

It didn't seem to Bobby that there was any occasion to make a scene. The other driver had been in the wrong, and if the damage was considerable he would have to pay. An inspection of the state of affairs, and an exchange of information and civilities, seemed all that was required. And if the driver proved to be a foreigner, one ought no doubt to be more forbearing still. But Giles Ashmore was of another mind. He was first out of the Mercedes, and addressing himself in tones of high indignation to what turned out to be the solitary occupant of the other car. If Giles wasn't exactly drunk he had no appearance of being entirely sober either. Perhaps a little artificial courage might be useful with his uncle. But it was being a nuisance now.

'Damn and blast you!' Giles was shouting robustly. 'Can't you see you're on the wrong side of the road? And what the hell are you doing here anyway? This is a private drive. You have no business here at all.'

'*Au contraire, mon vieux.*' Not unsurprisingly, the driver of the car with the French headlights was a Frenchman – a young Frenchman who had now descended to the road and was regarding Giles's surprise with some amusement. 'But this accident has been entirely my fault. It is your car, my dear Giles? It is a friend's? Happily the damage seems not severe. But the fullest reparation shall be made. Please introduce me, my dear fellow.'

'It's Jules – Jules de Voisin – the chap who's marrying my sister Virginia. Said to be some sort of relation, in a vague way.' Giles produced this in a graceless mutter, and then turned back to de Voisin. 'This is my friend Finn,' he said shortly, 'and a friend of Finn's called Bobby. It's Bobby's car you've buggered up.'

'Not exactly buggered up,' Bobby interposed – and wondered what de Voisin would make of this simple English colloquialism. 'A crumpled wing each. But I think we're both still mobile, and that's the main thing.'

'I am most relieved.' De Voisin responded instantly to this more civilized speech. 'And I reiterate my regrets. As to our good Giles's question about my business here, I have simply been visiting my kinsman, Martyn Ashmore –

whom you will know to be Giles's uncle. A visit *pour prendre congé*, as you English used to delight to say. I am shortly to go home for a while, and it appeared a necessary, as well as an agreeable, attention to pay. On my own behalf and Virginia's, my dear Giles. In fact I ventured to make my kinsman a small present – alike from Virginia and from myself.'

Finn, who had been prowling round both cars without taking any part in these exchanges, produced at this point a wild shout of laughter. That this smoothly spoken Frog had been up to precisely the same game as Giles was something which appeared to amuse him very much. He turned to Giles now.

'There's a tip for you,' he said. '*Finesse*, man! Tell your uncle that the grocer's claret is from you and the flat champagne from his Robina. From *your* Robina, I mean. Nothing's more likely to crown the success of your little venture. And now let's do another spot of the *congé* business with this chap, and get moving.'

Bobby – who was beginning to find something perplexing in Finn's attitude to their affair – agreed that they had better get on. They were already running late on any schedule that he had himself contemplated, and he didn't much want to arrive back at Long Dream with a noisy Finn in the small hours. So after satisfying himself with a decent solicitude that this night-wandering Frenchman's wretched car was in fact in running order, he exchanged addresses with him, and then shoved his two companions back into the Mercedes. The solitary Martyn Ashmore quite possibly kept very early hours. It would be extremely tedious if they had to get him out of bed. As he moved off, he glanced into his driving-mirror. De Voisin had shifted his car to its proper side of the road. But now he had got out again and was standing immobile beside it. There was no possibility of distinguishing his features, or even of being quite sure of the direction in which he was facing. But Bobby somehow imagined, without at all knowing why, that the young Frenchman was staring thoughtfully and even distrustfully after the three young Englishmen.

'Perhaps we ought to give it up.'

Bobby glanced sideways in surprise. It had been Giles who spoke, and something odd had sounded in the quality of his voice. Bobby wondered whether it was only a trick of the moonlight that made him look even paler than he had done at the end of dinner. Certainly there were beads of sweat on his brow. The filthy idiot is going to be sick, he told himself. He has no bloody head for liquor at all. And if he gets into his uncle's presence it will only be to make a complete botch of a plan that's feeble enough already.

'O.K. by me,' Bobby said. 'I'll call it a day, if you want to.'

'To hell with calling it a day – or a bleeding night either!' From the back of the Mercedes Finn produced this as an indignant shout. 'Giles has cold feet. But we're damned well going to see this through.'

'I haven't got cold feet, at all.' Giles managed a faint access of spirit. 'Only –' He hesitated, as if groping for something to say. 'It seems silly, somehow, now. After Virginia's young man doing the same thing.'

'He hasn't done the same thing. He's the only one to have done anything, so far, you stupid clot. So it's up to you to do something different. Give the gambit a different twist, old boy. Don't take a present in with you at all.' Finn appeared to view this as a sudden inspiration. 'Bobby and I will stay in the car, drinking up the claret. And we'll take your dreadful champagne back to Dream and feed it to Sir John's pigs.'

'I don't find that in the least funny. I don't –' At this point Giles Ashmore, who aspired to the refined employment of curating things in museums, *was* sick. Fortunately he did his vomiting more or less over the side of the car. And a few moments later – with a wan apologetic grin – he had sat back. 'Finn's right,' he said. 'Drive on.'

'I *am* driving on.' Bobby hadn't, in fact, thought it

necessary to slow down. 'You mean Finn's right about your blessed present? It's a forced note?'

'I don't know. I'll think. Just let's get to the Chase first.'

10

'It looks enormous,' Bobby said a few minutes later. Ashmore Chase was before them. The moonlight had turned its lichened roof to tarnished silver. The house might have been some scaly or plated creature slumbering on the bed of the ocean, its slender chimney-shafts the erected antennae which guarded its repose.

'It isn't, really,' Giles Ashmore said. 'It just sprawls around. Pull up for a minute, Bobby, and let's think.'

'Courage!' Finn said from the back.

'All right, all right – but I mustn't make a mistake, must I?' Giles stared dubiously at the darkened mansion. 'Anyway, I'm glad I've driven right up to the place, and not footed it along this drive, as one of you silly asses suggested.'

'You couldn't have footed it with your *petit cadeau*. I wonder, by the way, what that Frenchman's *petit cadeau* was? Nice night for a walk, apart from that.'

'There's Ibell to think of.'

'And who's Ibell, for the love of mike?'

'He's the keeper. About the only person Uncle Martyn has within a mile of him nowadays. He's said to prowl around the place at night with a shot-gun. Uncle Martyn gets nervy at times. It's something to do with not having had too good a war.'

'But this Ibell isn't going to shoot *you*.' Finn was impatient. 'If he's around, he'll simply sidle up respectfully, pulling his forelock to the squire's favourite nephew. That's right, isn't it, Bobby? You know the rural set-up in these things.'

'Absolutely right.' Bobby said this in a tone confessing

boredom. He had come to doubt whether there was much amusement in making fun of the rather feeble Giles Ashmore.

'But I'm *not* a favourite nephew. That's the whole point, isn't it? I have the job still to do. And as for Ibell, you just don't know him. Next to my other uncle – Ambrose Ashmore of Abbot's Yatter – Ibell is said to be the most ferocious character in the district.'

'Oh, rot!' Finn said. 'Even if he's a bleeding maniac, he can hardly shoot you down while you toy with your uncle's front-door bell. And now, listen. We'll drive right up. Bobby and I will help you to hump the Father Christmas stuff right into the porch or whatever. Then we'll turn round, and stop just out of sight round the first bend of the drive. Tell the old gentleman you were dropped by friends, and that they've ventured to take a moonlight stroll, and that you have a rendezvous with them in half an hour near the main road. That will give you a getaway.'

'I don't want you to go as far off as that.'

'We shan't, and you're not listening. We'll be no more than out of sight. But it will mean the old chap won't feel he has to ask Bobby and me in. Bobby, drive on.'

As these seemed to be rational arrangements, Bobby drove on. They appeared to have approached the Chase more or less by the back. But they rounded a corner, ran up some sort of ramp, and found themselves on a broad terrace.

'There's the main door,' Giles said. 'But – I say! – isn't the whole place in total darkness?'

'Not a bit of it,' Finn said cheerfully. 'We passed a ruddy great blazing window only five seconds ago. You must be as blind as a bat. Out you get.' Finn jumped from the car. 'And heave out the good cheer. Bobby and I will watch you ring the bell, old chap, and then we'll cut and run.' Finn gave one of his sudden and disconcerting laughs. It sounded very loud in the dark. 'I've just remembered a funny thing.' He turned to Bobby. 'It was when we were talking about just this: Giles's ringing the front-door bell at the Chase. Your father said that Giles should first take out a life assurance policy. Seems to make the place a kind of Castle Dangerous, wouldn't you say? Childe Roland to the dark tower came.'

'It *is* dark,' Giles said. He seemed to be in a panic again. 'I think we've made a mistake.'

'Too late, old chap.' With another burst of unholy laughter, Finn stepped forward and tugged the bell. 'Run, Bobby you bastard!' he shouted, and made a dash for the car.

Bobby followed briskly. He had a notion Finn cherished designs on the wheel of the Mercedes, which was something which, during the remainder of this nocturnal escapade, he wasn't going to have. After Finn had drunk a certain amount, he appeared to have the faculty of going on getting drunker for some hours, absolutely *gratis*. It must be economically advantageous. But it didn't go with making free with a friend's car.

'This is boring,' Finn said, twenty minutes later. He was sitting beside Bobby, and had smoked several cigarettes. 'But at least there's more joy to come.'

'What do you mean – more joy to come?' Bobby heard a note of suspicion in his own voice. He was beginning to think it time to be getting off to bed.

'You'll see. This is going to turn out even funnier than it was meant to be. Only I'm surprised the aged relative is detaining our Giles so long.'

'We said half an hour. Do you mean something should have happened to send Giles out on his ear before that?' It seemed to Bobby that a kind of malice was building up in Finn. He had almost forgotten that Finn had been Giles's rival for the hand of the agreeable but impecunious Robina Bunker. For the first time that night, he wondered whether there were, so to speak, wheels within wheels in this business. 'Finn, are you playing this straight?' Bobby asked.

'Just what do you mean by that?'

'You and this Giles both having been after the girl. Are you really backing Giles now?'

'You're crazy! What else could I be doing – boiling over with a passion for revenge? I ask you Bobby, am I that sort of chap?'

Bobby – consulting his professional knowledge of human nature – decided that Finn was not that sort of chap. Finn was just a silly ass, and entirely bearable as such from time to time.

'You're a silly ass,' Bobby said. 'And, of course, I'm very fond of you.'

'Exactly! So we've got that clear. Hullo! I think he's coming now.'

A flicker of light from the invisible house had suggested the opening and closing of the front door. A moment later, they heard Giles Ashmore's footsteps. Then he swung round the first bend of the drive, walking briskly. He raised an arm and gave a wave; the gesture brought his hand up out of shadow and into moonlight; it was like the sudden pale flame of a candle, Bobby told himself.

'Absolutely O.K.!' Giles almost shouted as he came up. He was a man transformed. 'I knew I'd bring it off, whatever you said. And I have.'

'Your uncle will stump up!' Bobby asked.

'I'm sure he will. He was touched. And he'll *be* touched.' Giles laughed appreciatively at his own joke. 'It's just a matter of the amount, I'd say. But at the moment, by the way, he wants –'

'You told him what your application was in aid of?' Finn interrupted. He sounded incredulous. 'The bedding of Miss Bunker – all that?'

'Yes, of course.'

Finn gave his yell of laughter. 'I'd like to meet Uncle Martyn Ashmore. He's a deep one, he is.'

'Well, you're not going to – not now. But Bobby is.' Giles talked rapidly and in plain excitement. 'Bobby, he wants you just to come back and be introduced. Something about having met your father, and worked it out that you must be a great-nephew of his old friend Somebody Raven.'

'Everard Raven. You mean your uncle wants this handshake now?' Bobby was surprised. 'The idea was –'

'You don't mind, do you? And Finn won't mind waiting. We'll only be a jiffy.'

'But I want to come too!' Finn was extremely indignant. 'You mean I'm to stay in the car as unpresentable? What a damned uncivil thing!'

'Not unpresentable – only tight.' Giles – he was really a transformed Giles – brought this out briskly. 'Come on, Bobby. Five minutes will do the trick.'

Finn made a resigned gesture, and lit another cigarette. Bobby followed Giles back to the house. He was trying to remember all he could about his great-uncle Everard. He had a notion that he had edited an encyclopaedia, and was not to be confused with Ranulph Raven, the author of *Tales: Chiefly Imaginative or Grotesque*. Ranulph Raven, too, had presumably been acquainted with sundry Ashmores. Perhaps he had picked up a grotesque tip or two from them.

'Giles,' Bobby said, 'you did honestly come clean to your uncle about Robina?'

'Yes, of course. It's the whole point, isn't it? But, by the way, I don't think you should mention her to him yourself. He'd probably like to think our engagement wasn't public property until after he'd approved it.'

'I don't see that it's your uncle's business to approve of your engagement – except, I suppose, that he's going to finance the marriage. But I'll say nothing about it unless he does. This really must be just five minutes, wouldn't you say?'

'Oh, certainly. I'll ring the bell again.'

But this proved unnecessary. The door opened as Giles stepped forward, and revealed to Bobby's curiosity – although for the moment only in silhouette against some bleak and unshaded light in the background – the craggy figure of Martyn Ashmore. Bobby decided that the proprietor of the Chase was older than he had expected – and then found himself deciding that he was younger. What led to this instant conflict of impressions – if indeed it wasn't entirely random – he couldn't quite make out.

'Ah, Giles, come in again.' Martyn Ashmore stepped back; the two young men advanced; Giles politely closed his kinsman's front door behind him. 'And this must be Robert? How do you do. I have told Giles that your great-uncle Everard was a close friend of mine. A remarkable man. A very hard-working man. His *Revised and Enlarged Resurrection* was a masterpiece.'

'I'm afraid I haven't heard of it, sir.' Bobby was rather startled by this sudden vision of a deceased kinsman in so apocalyptic a role.

'The dictionary he undertook after his *New Millennium*. That, you know, was his encyclopaedia. Your father fell over the wall of my park.' Martyn Ashmore appeared unaware that here was a transition of some abruptness. 'I was very glad to meet him. Turned out an authority on portraiture. Jarvis, Haydon – fellows of that sort.'

Bobby contrived to produce some suitable reply to this. He was accustomed to thinking of his father as a notable polymath. And what his father didn't know about, his mother did. Perhaps this was why Bobby had taken to fiction, which is a field of knowledge only in a somewhat special sense. Meantime, he had an opportunity to glance round this strange old man's habitat. Its first suggestion was extremely comfortless. The hall, although not large, had a flagged floor, a raftered ceiling, a random display of rusty weapons on its walls, and a certain amount of useless-looking Tudor furniture standing around. There was a disproportionately large fireplace, and in this there dully shone, like a glow-worm in the mouth of some forbidding cavern, the single bar of a small and extremely primitive electric fire. The whole set-up, moreover, had a mouldy smell.

It wasn't altogether apparent, however, that the Ashmores had to suffer, as head of the family, a savage old person lost to all the decencies or even creature comforts of life. Mr Ashmore's black trousers had here and there a greenish hue, but there was a suggestion that they had been donned, together with an appropriate change of linen, at some prescribed evening hour. His faded velvet smoking-jacket seemed really to belong to an age in which gentlemen veritably put on a special garment of the sort before lighting a cigar. Perhaps what Bobby could glimpse through a half-open door was in fact a smoking-room, and at least it had a bright log fire burning in a sizeable grate. Through another door, it was true, there was visible a once dignified apartment which seemed to have been roughly adapted to the uses of a kitchen, and there was everywhere a little more dust than seemed compatible with the existence of any indoor servants whatever. It was towards the first of these doors that Mr Ashmore now made a move. He seemed to be proposing, if not some form of material refreshment, at least the enjoyment of the young men's conversation for a few minutes longer.

'I think we'd better not stay, Uncle Martyn,' Giles said. Giles's manner had become nervous again. It was as if, knowing he had pulled off a wonderful *coup* with this all-important relative, he was feeling that it would be wise to go while the going was good. Perhaps he was afraid that Bobby would somehow put his foot in it. 'Bobby has a friend we have to pick up,' he went on, 'and then I have to be dropped at home and they go on to Dream.'

'Then I must not detain you.' Martyn Ashmore, it struck Bobby, was speaking to them rather as a grown-up speaks to well-bred children – as if to contemporaries, but with a faint playfulness at the same time. And his nephew Giles he definitely found amusing. This emerged in the next words he spoke. 'I must simply retire to the enjoyment, my dear lad, of your very original present. You have really surprised me, I am bound to say. Shall I ever surprise you? It seems too much for an old man to hope for. To impose the unexpected upon one's intimates – even upon one's mere relations – holds a peculiar pleasure. Don't you agree?'

'Well, yes – I do.' Giles produced this rather uncertainly. But suddenly he reiterated it. 'Yes. I do.'

'There was a fellow who wrote plays' – Martyn Ashmore had turned to Bobby – 'and, as it happens, I was mentioning him to your father the other day. He said something to the effect that the tables of consanguinity are founded upon a basis of natural revulsion. It may be I don't get the words right, but the idea is clear. I have always subscribed to it, so far as my own consanguinity is concerned. I detest all other Ashmores – and it has worried me that, as a matter of mere decorum, I may have to part my possessions among them. Upon the occasion of my death, that is. And my death might now take place, you know, in little more than thirty years time. Or so statistics and the habits of heredity suggest to me. But what was I saying? Ah, yes. I detest all Ashmores, and it is therefore reasonable to infer that all Ashmores detest me. Suddenly an Ashmore appears, bearing gifts. Have I any reason to distrust him? We sport no Grecian ancestry, so far as I know. Giles, you follow me?'

'I *don't* quite follow you, Uncle.' Giles's uneasiness was increasing. 'I'm sure I never heard anything about Greek marriages in our family. Only some French ones, and I don't –'

'*Timeo Danaos et dona ferentes*. I see that Bobby understands me. He is clearly a ripe scholar. But now I see that you must really go. Mr Appleby, please give my best wishes to your father. But for the fact that I rarely venture abroad, I would call on him, and hope to be presented to your mother.' Martyn Ashmore, as he moved through these ritual remarks, moved also towards his front door. It swung open under his hand. 'And so, good night,' he said. 'And, Giles, I shall be thinking about you, and about what we have talked over earlier. Who knows what will come of it? You may – yes, after all – you may be surprised.'

11

Finn was standing on the terrace. He had got tired of waiting in the car, and had been taking a prowl round the house, the sickle moon was now high in the sky. But light cloud was drifting across it, and the broken façade of the ancient building gleamed and darkened alternately like a stage-set defectively lit.

'I took a peep,' Finn called out as they came up. His voice sounded much too loud in the still night. 'But I didn't see any sign of you. Didn't the old fellow crack one of those bottles of champagne?'

'What do you mean – you took a peep?' Giles demanded. 'Have you been peering through a keyhole?'

'That lighted window, you idiot.' Finn pointed along the terrace. 'There's a curtain not quite drawn, and it seems to be the old gentleman's sitting-room. But he must have been palavering with you somewhere else.'

'We didn't go beyond the hall,' Bobby said. 'And now I think it's time we cleared out. Let's get back to the car.'

'I wonder whether he *has* opened a bottle of that wine?' Giles asked. Uncertainty again seemed to have overtaken him. 'He has an odd way of talking sometimes. Courtly and old-world, I suppose. And he said something about enjoying what I'd brought along. Let's have a look.'

'For pity's sake!' Bobby said. He was suddenly feeling impatient over this whole affair. But Giles had already moved the short distance down the terrace, and Finn was skipping gleefully after him. Bobby hesitated, and then followed.

'He isn't!' Giles whispered, and drew back from a quick glance he had taken through the half-drawn curtains. Bobby said nothing, but made a similar brief inspection. It was the room with the fire which had been visible from the hall, and Martyn Ashmore was sitting in an easy-chair at one side of the fireplace. Bobby saw him put out a hand to a small table and pick up a book. There was certainly no bottle or glass in evidence.

'He was merely saying something polite,' Finn said. 'Probably he doesn't drink at all, and will send your blessed *cadeau* to a church sale.' Finn's voice was again recklessly loud. 'It's not quite the Christmas season yet,' he added. 'But what about striking up with a carol?'

'Be quiet, you fool,' Bobby said. 'And if you both want to come away in my car, come now. This prowling and spying –'

But Bobby's sentence – plainly to be framed in a key of moral reprobation – never got itself finished. It was interrupted by an angry voice from the near-darkness below the terrace.

'Stay where you are!' the voice shouted roughly. 'If you run, I'll fire!'

'Run!' Bobby hissed. He was clear he wasn't going to take an order like that. 'Into the park. Draw him away from the car.'

'It's Ibell!' Already fleeing down the terrace, Giles produced this in a panicky gasp. 'He's quite –'

But Giles's sentence didn't get itself finished either. There was a loud report, accompanied by the unbelievable sound of a patter of lead on the wall of the house close behind them. The ferocious Ibell – if it was indeed he – not being in a position to fire a shot across their bow, had fired one manically close to their stern.

'Scatter!' Bobby shouted. And he ran to the edge of the terrace and jumped. At once a dramatic darkness engulfed him, so that for an alarming moment he wondered whether his blind leap had taken him to the bottom of a well. Then he realized that it had merely been synchronous with the moon's making a dive into deeper cloud than hitherto. With a madman around, this was all to the good.

He had fallen soft – into a drift of beech-leaves, with leaf-mould underneath. He put up a hand and removed a dry twig from his hair. He could still faintly hear running footsteps. Suddenly he heard, too, the baying of a hound. But no – he didn't. It wasn't a hound. It was Finn. And his heart warmed to Finn, whose involvement in this night's proceedings was not, like Giles Ashmore's, mercenary, but entirely joyous and freakish. And now the hound abruptly – so to speak – took to the air. It too-whitted and too-whooed. Finn, like the boy so movingly recalled by Wordsworth, was blowing mimic hootings to the owls. But the keeper – if it was the keeper – appeared not assuaged by this gamesome metamorphosis. There was a further angry shout, and the shot-gun went off again. If the chap was really firing into darkness – if he was letting off his bleeding weapon other than straight into air – he deserved to be locked up. Even if he believed himself to have stumbled upon a trio of burglars on his employer's terrace, he was far from entitled to try and maim somebody.

The racket didn't appear to have brought Martyn Ashmore out of the house. Perhaps he was accustomed to Ibell's behaving in this way during his nocturnal perambulations. Perhaps he was just absorbed in his book. But that was unimportant. The main point seemed to be that, like Bobby himself, Giles and Finn had, for the present, got clean away. Particularly if the moon continued covered, there was really very little that Ibell could do in the way of running to earth any one of three young men in prudent hiding in a large park. Unless, of course, Finn started fooling again. Or unless Ibell, if so minded, could summon a *real* Hound of the Baskervilles to his aid. Only Bobby's car was a difficulty. If Ibell was aware of its presence, as he well might be, he had only to lurk near it to make a fair cop later on. Fortunately the car was in deep darkness a hundred yards down the drive. Bobby decided to wait for ten minutes or so, and then make his way cautiously in its direction. Perhaps they would find themselves making a rendezvous there, all three, and manage a successful get-away.

If that was at all the proper thing to do. Bobby Appleby, whose intellectual interests and literary pursuits didn't much alter the fact that he was a very correct young man, found himself not at all sure about this. The whole evening's adventure had been a plot of sorts directed against Martyn Ashmore – and looked at other than in irresponsible high spirits it had been a plot of rather an unworthy kind. And the further business of peering through that window – which was what the keeper had virtually caught them at – was something that, as between gentlemen, ought simply not to have been on.

This upsurge of what Bobby himself would scoffingly have called *sahib*-stuff upset Bobby a good deal. Perhaps the only correct course was to walk up to the house again – risking a few pellets in one's backside – and ring that damned bell and apologize and explain. They ought all three to do that. But if the other two weren't now contactable, and this was Bobby's own honest conviction, then Bobby ought to do it off his own bat.

Bobby didn't. What he reckoned as ten minutes went by, and he had made no move to do anything of the kind. And the reason, he found, was a very odd one. It had something to do with old Mr Martyn Ashmore himself. There had been something equivocal – a good literary word – in Ashmore's attitude during the brief epilogue – so to speak – to his encounter with his nephew which Bobby had been called in to witness. To put it vulgarly, the proprietor of Ashmore Chase had in some obscure fashion been laughing up his sleeve. In language yet more demotic, he had been pleasing himself with the knowledge that his designing nephew Giles would presently be laughing on the other side of his face.

At this point Bobby Appleby found himself feeling in a pocket for his pipe. He checked himself as he did so – the flare of a match would be just one more folly – and probably without reflecting on the truth of Finn's assertion that he was his father's son. But at least his father had confessed to him that a good part of his policeman's career had been built on hunches, and that hunches were always the better of being controlled by a meditative smoke. This present drift of an odd persuasion through his own mind was eminently a hunch. He could give himself no rational account of it. There was, for instance, only further perplexity in his awareness that it was bound up with something sensed in the hinterland of Finn's more recent posture in the affair. For what was Finn but a silly ass? Nothing at all, Bobby told himself. He almost spoke the words aloud.

He suddenly found that he was looking at the smooth shaft of a beech – the tree, presumably, amid the fallen leaves of which he had tumbled. In other words, the moon was in business again. He listened intently, and all he heard was the hooting of an owl. He had no difficulty in distinguishing between a real owl and a mimic one. (Real owls, if Wordsworth was to be believed, did have – which shows that an anti-novelist is cleverer than an owl.) Some sort of proper nocturnal order was establishing itself again in the purlieus of Ashmore Chase. It seemed a hint that the best that three young idiots could do was to clear out.

Bobby heaved himself out of shadow – absurdly enough, it took quite a nerve – and walked in the direction of the drive.

Two indistinguishable figures stood beside the car. They might, for all Bobby knew, be a couple of constables, summoned by an Ibell who had come to a better mind. Which could mean that, the next morning, Sir John Appleby would be faced with the job of offering tactful explanations to Colonel Thomas Pride. Boys will be boys. Still scarcely more than undergraduates. That sort of thing. Mr Robert Appleby (author of a promising first novel called *The Lumber Room*) found himself not liking this idea at all. However, the figures turned out to be Finn and Giles.

Giles looked pretty ghastly – so much so that Bobby found himself wondering whether his was a backside that was really half an ounce or so heavier than it had been fifteen minutes ago. But probably it was only funk. A young man whose ambition it was to snuggle into some womb-like museum or gallery for life was probably not apt for wild doings in the dark.

'Pile in,' Bobby said curtly. 'Pile in, and I'll start the car. That chap –'

He broke off – as one was apt to do when Finn produced one of those lunatic laughs. But there had been another sound as well. It had come from Giles, and it could be described only as a snarl. Bobby suddenly perceived that this tiresome evening had produced yet another annoyance. Finn and Giles were in the middle of a violent quarrel.

'Stimied!' Finn turned and hurled this at Bobby in a kind of mad glee. 'Giles is stimied. And the old fox is preparing to ply his niblick in the bunker. Robina Bunker. Hooray!'

'Stop it, Finn. You're behaving like an idiot. And rather a nasty idiot, at that.' Bobby's patience had suddenly vanished. 'I don't know what you're talking about. And I don't think I want to.'

'You're a prig, Bobby Appleby. All Applebys are prigs. And as for Giles, he's a kind of cuckold. Uncle Martyn has booked the Bunker. It's in *The Times*. I saw it in the pub.'

'You're a bloody liar!' Giles advanced rather indecisively upon Finn. 'A bloody liar and a horrid cad.' Giles's fury was not impressive. He might have been about to stick his fists in his eyes and blubber.

'I thought we were going to have the fun of seeing Giles

kicked out,' Finn said. 'But the old chap played it cooler than that. He sat back and laughed at his youthful rival. He's toasting his toes, and drinking Giles's confusion in Giles's own champagne at this moment, I expect. It's the funniest thing I've ever met.'

'Finn, I've had enough of you.' Bobby had stepped between his two companions. 'If Martyn Ashmore has really got this girl to agree to marry him it seems to me a pretty poor show. I don't see anything particularly lovely about your pal Giles's behaviour, but that doesn't mean you're not going to shut up.'

'Prig. Sir Prig, Lady Prig, and Baby Bobby Prig. All the Applebys.'

'If you say part of that again, Finn, I'll knock you down. It's a promise. And I can.'

'You can't take a ruddy joke, either of you. I'm off, if I have to sleep under a hedge.'

'We're being silly.' Bobby found it took a good deal of self-control to say this. 'We'd better begin to –'

He was talking, so far as Finn was concerned, to empty air. The violent young man had turned, swung down the drive, and vanished into darkness.

12

'I never knew Finn behave quite like that.' As he said this to Giles Ashmore, Bobby realized how completely Giles Ashmore was a stranger to him. Whereas Finn he had known quite some time. Finn and he had been at private school together. 'Why should he pick a quarrel with me? That's pretty well what he was up to.' Bobby peered at Giles, and even in the near darkness still didn't like the look of him. 'Get into the car,' he said abruptly. 'Perhaps Finn will be waiting at the top of the drive.'

'I can't believe it.' Giles climbed into the car as he had been told – heavily, as if he were an old man. 'About Robina and my uncle.'

'You're sure you made it clear to him about your engagement to this girl?'

'Of course. I've said so already.'

'And he didn't bat an eyelid?'

'No. He congratulated me. The filthy old swine!'

'Do you think' – Bobby started the engine of the Mercedes and slipped into gear – 'that perhaps Finn has made it up? About the announcement in *The Times*? He seems to be fit for anything at the moment – just for the sake of a nasty laugh.' Bobby, who was feeling sorry for the wretched Giles and the collapse of his miserable little plan, offered this suggestion without much conviction. 'And how could your uncle have got all that way with Robina? How can he even have been continuing to see her?'

'He's what Finn said – deep. And it's rather a thing in my family: marrying a young girl in one's disgusting old age. Knocking her up, too. Kids around the place who might be one's great-grandchildren.' Giles paused disconsolately as the car gathered speed on the drive. 'As for being able to chase up Robina, you never know what my uncle is up to. There are all sorts of queer stories about him. There's one about some French people wanting to kill him because of something he did in that rotten old war. My father says that anything of that kind is all nonsense, and merely shows that Uncle Martyn is off his head. But I don't at all know.'

'It doesn't seem terribly relevant, anyway – not to your affair.'

'I suppose not. But there's another thing. He's supposed to be more or less a recluse, never leaving the Chase. But who knows?' Giles again paused broodingly. 'The old sod could skip up to town twice a week – couldn't he? – without anybody being any the wiser.'

'No doubt he could.' Bobby had come to a halt at the head of the drive. There was no sign of Finn. The silly ass had simply walked out of the landscape. Bobby was annoyed to think that, on the following morning, he would have to tell his parents that their guest had departed in a huff. His annoyance made him turn rather sharply on Giles. 'Are you really upset about this?' he asked.

'Certainly I'm upset.'

'Let's get this clear. Have you known that Robina is this sort of girl, or haven't you?'

'What do you mean – this sort of girl?'

'For pity's sake!' Bobby got into motion again rather abruptly. 'If Finn's story is true, Miss Bunker has ditched you, without a word spoken, in favour of your rich uncle – and your rather old rich uncle, at that. I'm asking whether you did, or did not, know that this girl you were proposing to marry is a ghastly little bitch?'

'I don't think you should speak like that about Robina.'

'I'm not speaking about her, as you call it. I'm just asking for information, and I'm sorry if I hurt your feelings. But my curiosity isn't all that intense, anyway. I'll drive you home to King's Yatter now. And that will be that.'

'I don't want to go home.'

Bobby shoved at the accelerator. This, he thought, was a bit too much. Perhaps Giles Ashmore expected to be taken back to Dream – as a kind of exchange for Finn – and have his hand held through the night.

'I want to go to London,' Giles said. 'Now.'

'What on earth do you want to go to London for?'

'That's where she is. Robina. I've got to have it out with her.'

'Well, I'm all in favour of that.' Bobby's opinion of his companion rose a little. 'But why not go back to the Chase, and have it out with your uncle first? If he has really pinched your girl and kept mum about it you should jolly well tell him what you think. You might even ask for your champagne and claret back.'

'I don't think I'd care to do that, somehow.' Giles appeared to have taken Bobby's suggestion quite seriously. 'I don't think I want to see Uncle Martyn again, at all. I've told you what I want to do. To go to London. Now.'

Bobby swore to himself. It wouldn't have been decent to do so aloud. Whatever was to be thought of Giles Ashmore, the poor bastard had been given a raw deal, and it wouldn't do just to let him down now. Yet Bobby didn't much kindle to the notion of driving the rejected young lover through the night – and even perhaps being involved in some distressing scene with the faithless Miss Bunker herself.

'I'll drive you to town,' Bobby said.

'That's very decent of you.' Giles's tone was unengagingly perfunctory, but at least his words were those that ought to have been spoken. 'It will be pretty cold in the small hours in a car like this.'

This addendum, naturally enough, didn't greatly take Bobby's fancy. He had to resist a temptation to come abruptly to a halt – and not to move again until he had the Mercedes to himself.

'I'm not sure there isn't a decent night train that stops at Linger Junction. Will you please drive there, and we'll see?'

'As a matter of fact, I know there is.' Bobby suddenly felt more cheerful. 'Five past midnight, and Paddington first stop. You'd be there a lot quicker than if we drove. Not that three o'clock in the morning is too cheerful a time to arrive.'

'I shouldn't be feeling cheerful, anyway.'

'I suppose not.' Bobby felt rather touched by this naïve remark. 'Have you got enough money for a ticket?'

'I think so. But of course there's breakfast before the banks open. Can you lend me five pounds?'

'Not many breakfasts for one cost five pounds. I can lend you thirty bob.'

'That's very decent of you,' Giles Ashmore said. This time, he spoke frankly as a much injured man. 'I expect I can make it do.'

The very grandest trains quite often stopped at Linger Junction. The effect was of a kind of slumming. Through the plate-glass windows of well-appointed Pullman carriages, and while toying with the delicious viands which only British Railways can provide, the better class of traveller would gaze out appalled upon the drab and often dripping or drizzling scene. Linger itself was scarcely visible. It was nearly a mile away, and architecturally not of a character much to impress itself even upon a middle distance. Prominently in view however were the Station Hotel (on one side of the main line) and the New Station Hotel (on the other). Nomenclature alone readily distinguished these gaunt and hideous structures, since both were a product of the same unaesthetic decade – one inordinately dedicated, one had to feel, to an optimistic vision of what the progress of steam locomotion was likely to achieve for this slumberous part of England. And slumber of a sort dominated the branch line, as it was flanked by a large and seemingly abandoned cemetery. In the angle between the lines there was a muddy yard in which buses manoeuvred and cars could be parked – the latter gratuitously but with dubious legality. The law-abiding and nervous used a sort of corral to which access was gained merely by presenting the snout of one's vehicle before an electronically controlled barrier. This death-ray species of contrivance was the Junction's triumph of modernity. When you wanted to get out again you shoved two shillings into a slot. But this was commonly less productive of any immediate result. Young Gregory Grope (whose father had been an engine-driver, but who had himself come down in the world and was the Junction's only porter) was frequently to be observed by the passing traveller as painfully at labour upon some entirely primitive cranking device which had been thoughtfully provided by the manufacturers as a last resort in extreme emergency. There was also a tin shed labelled 'Grand Junction Garage: Complete Overhauls', and a derelict pump from which the proprietor of this establishment had once aspired to dispense cut-price petrol.

It was drizzling when Bobby pulled up. Remarking the unpromising pump, he glanced nervously at the appropriate gauge before switching off his engine. It appeared not improbable that while Giles Ashmore was speeding towards London and the false Robina in the night he himself would be dossing down in the back of the Mercedes in some god-forsaken lay-by.

'There's going to be rather a long wait,' Giles said grumpily.

'Well, yes – I'm afraid so. But perhaps you'll find a waiting-room that's been left open. It may even have a stove.'

'We can go and look. I'll buy your platform-ticket.'

'My dear chap, you don't expect me to see you on your train, and tuck you up in your corner?'

'I'd like you to, please.' Giles suddenly sounded quite humble. 'I know it's silly, but I have a thing about railway-stations. Particularly about platforms. I'm afraid of throwing myself in front of a train.'

'There won't be a train – not until your own comes in.'

'That's the one I'd be afraid of. I used to think it had something to do with reading *Anna Karenina* at an impressionable age. Have you read *Anna Karenina*? It's by Tolstoi.'

'Yes, oddly enough I have read *Anna Karenina*.'

'Then you remember what happened to her. But actually it turned out not to be about *Anna Karenina* at all. I had an analyst once, and he worked it out for me. It seems there's something called separation-anxiety. You have it when about to set out on a journey.'

'No, I don't.'

'People do, I mean. And I do. I wish you'd stay. It would be awfully decent of you, Billy. Bobby, that is.'

Bobby took a deep breath, and then climbed out of the car. He might have been described as in the grip of his code. The evident truth was that the events of the last couple of hours had been altogether too much for this wretched creature. Probably the demented Ibell and his slugs had scared the lights out of him. And in London, after all, he was facing a rotten sort of show.

'All right,' Bobby said. 'But what about the other end? Shall you be able to beat it out of Paddington rapidly? Without, I mean, being hypnotized by those gleaming and evil lines of metal?'

'Oh, yes. I know you haven't much to do – but it's nice of you to offer to come the whole way, all the same. But the other end of a journey is quite different. My analyst said –'

Bobby Appleby, although not an emotional youth,

heard himself interrupt this with a kind of strangled cry.

'Very well,' he said. 'Let's get on the platform, and see how we can pass the time. There may be something to distract you. One of those machines that bellow your weight at you. Or that you punch out names on to tack on your tuck-box or your toy-cupboard.'

'There's no occasion to be rude,' Giles Ashmore said.

Part Four

A Call at King's Yatter

13

'I don't know when Bobby got in last night,' Appleby said, and poured himself a cup of coffee. 'He does at least have the art of getting himself to bed without making a row. The same can't be said for his friend Finn.'

'It was Finn, was it? I rather thought I heard you going to investigate something or other.' Judith Appleby flicked the toast-machine into action. 'He didn't come back along with Bobby?'

'No – and I think it was long after. In what one might call the not so small small hours. He got lost at the back of the house, and I went down to see what was happening. We had quite a chat.'

'A chat! It seems an odd time for it. Was he tight?'

'He had been, and he no longer was. Or that was my impression. He had been drinking, but not after closing-time. He was extremely apologetic. Not about drinking, but because he'd had some sort of row with Bobby. Frightfully bad form, he said, when staying with a chap's parents.'

'I quite agree. But perhaps Bobby was being rather tiresomely superior towards his simple friends.'

'Possibly so.' Appleby felt a little irritated by this remark. 'But the boy can't help having brains, you know.'

'No, indeed. He never had a chance.' Judith was amused. 'Finn came back on his own?'

'Yes. He got a couple of lifts, he says, from Ashmore Chase.'

'The Chase!' Judith's hand was suddenly suspended over the marmalade pot. 'What on earth was this boy Finn doing there?'

'They were all three there. Don't you remember? Taking an irresistible gift of St Emilion or Médoc to Martyn Ashmore – who happens to be sitting on what must be one of the best small private cellars left in England.' Appleby checked himself in the midst of frankly juvenile laughter. 'I oughtn't to have let them do it, I suppose – since I'd happened to get a glimpse of that cellar only the other day. But it seemed rather touching and absurd, and I let them go ahead. The old man's nephew – I don't recall his name –'

'Giles.'

'Giles was proposing to ingratiate himself with his uncle in a mildly funny fashion, don't you think? I felt they ought to play the comedy out.'

'And did they?'

'That's what young Finn wanted to tell me about. But when it hadn't come all that clear in half an hour, I told him to go to bed. I provided him, by the way, with a pint of milk from the fridge.'

'Then there won't be any for their breakfast. And none for Hoobin's cocoa either.'

'I expect Hoobin still has some of his birthday whisky to fall back on, and the young gentleman probably won't stir until lunchtime.'

'Just what did you gather happened at the Chase?'

'It all seems to have been a little odd. Think of the unexpected element in the comedy: the aged Ashmore's incredible engagement to his nephew's beloved Roberta.'

'Robina.'

'Yes, Robina Fairway.'

'Bunker.'

'That's right – Bunker. They hadn't a clue about it, just as I supposed. But Finn came on it while they were waiting to have dinner in some pub. He kept mum. He didn't want to spoil the joke.'

'I call that uncharitable, John. Or childish – like your letting them go ahead with the wine.'

'You're absolutely right. And, later on, Finn was to reproach himself.'

'That at least was something. You're taking a long time to tell me how the foolish business turned out.'

'Finn took a long time too. Perhaps his recollection is poor because he was a bit fuddled. He was also uneasy. There were things at the Chase he didn't like. It seems they ran into that young Frenchman, de Voisin, who was coming away from the house. He too may be judged to have designs on Martyn Ashmore's cheque-book, since he's engaged to Giles's sister. Finn believes himself to have sensed something odd about him. But that wasn't all. Giles staggered into the Chase with his load of bourgeois wine, and emerged reporting that his uncle had received him – complete with his story about Robina – very well. Nothing was said about old Martyn's conflicting matrimonial project. Giles took Bobby back to have a word with his uncle, and Finn felt annoyed at being left out in the cold. The Robina business was probably rankling with him too. He had been yet another suitor, remember, of the fascinating lady. So he started playing the fool. But only after something mildly alarming had occurred. It seems that Martyn Ashmore's keeper – a fellow called Ibell – turned up, and started taking pot shots at our three young worthies in the dark.'

'At Bobby?' Lady Appleby wasn't at all amused.

'At Bobby's behind, and Giles's behind, and Finn's behind – or more probably at a safe but still intimidating remove from these targets. It's something a keeper will occasionally do, when poachers or marauders are around. Nobody was hurt.'

'The young idiots!' Judith said. She took a deep breath, and poured herself a second cup of coffee. 'And then, I suppose, they went skylarking about the landscape in that lethal car.'

'Not exactly. All this was a bit odd. But Finn, on his own showing, then behaved more oddly still. I didn't really get the hang of it. He seems suddenly to have persuaded himself that there was something positively sinister in the background of the whole affair. So he had this row with Bobby. Not an honest row. He deliberately picked a quarrel with him, and so contrived to go off on his own.'

'I'm not sure that Finn himself doesn't sound a bit sinister.'

'I agree. Or at least he was putting himself in what might be called a vulnerable position, if there was really any kind of dirty work afoot at the Chase.'

'But how could there be? It's absurd!'

'Don't forget my own adventure there.'

There was a moment's silence across the Applebys' breakfast table.

'That French boy was around on both occasions,' Judith said.

'Very true. And on the second occasion somebody else proved to be around as well. A new entrant among our *dramatis personae*. It seems –' Appleby broke off suddenly, for the door of the breakfast-room had opened. 'Good morning,' he said politely. 'I hope you slept well?'

Only Finn's head and shoulders were visible for a moment. They had the appearance of being poised for instant withdrawal were the marmalade pot to come flying at his head.

'Good morning,' Judith said. 'The coffee is still quite hot, and Mrs Colpoys will have something in the oven. But I'm afraid there isn't much milk.'

'Oh, I say!' With visible effort, Finn entered the room. 'Lady Appleby, I am most frightfully sorry. Coming in like that and disturbing Sir John. I don't know how to apologize.' He glanced round apprehensively. 'Is Bobby up yet?'

'Not yet. You probably know that Bobby is quite easy to make one's peace with. Please sit down and relax.'

'Yes, of course. I mean, thanks most awfully. Has Sir John told you all about it?'

'Up to a point. The *pièce de résistance* in your Bar-
mecidal banquet was yet to come. I'm not sure that John
had quite got hold of it when you parted for the night – or
for the morning.'

'Well, no – I suppose not.' Finn looked nervously at
Appleby, who had risen to ring a bell. It was an action
which appeared susceptible of misinterpretation. 'I say,'
Finn said, 'are you going to have me ushered out? I jolly
well deserve –'

'Your bacon and whatever,' Appleby murmured. 'But
Mrs Colpoys has heard you already, and here it is.'

Finn received his breakfast with dumb gratitude; he
seemed surprised that it was set before him by the
Appleby's house-keeper without visible disapprobation.
His experiences of the previous night, however trying,
had not spoilt his appetite. But he possessed considerable
skill – no doubt acquired through long practice – in eating and talking simultaneously and with an equal rapid-
ity. Occasionally he waved a knife or fork vigorously in
front of him. He was coming, in fact, to feel quite at home
again.

'You see,' he said, 'I was very puzzled by myself. And it's
not at all a common thing with me. I mean, you know,
that I've never reckoned myself to be what they call an
introspective type. Would I be wrong there, do you
think?'

'I'd hardly suppose so.' Appleby passed the toast-rack.
'But,' he added gravely, 'our acquaintance has scarcely
been of long duration.'

'That's true, of course. But there I was, finding I'd got
thoroughly worried about something I couldn't pin down,
and with a queer feeling that I wanted to be alone. Alone
to think, you see, although as a matter of fact I don't do a
great deal of thinking in a general way. I even felt there
was something I wanted to investigate, although I hadn't
a notion what it was. Have you ever felt like that, sir?'

'Frequently,' Appleby said. 'But please go on.'

'Well, that was why I had a row with Bobby and just

walked off. Quite soon after that, Bobby and Giles must have driven away. And I came out of hiding, more or less, and wandered up and down that drive for quite a bit, wondering what on earth had come over me. I don't think I was particularly tight any longer. You see I'd been putting on quite an act as a shouting hare-brained idiot, and that's a thing that burns up the alk, if you ask me, and sobers a chap up quite quickly. Lady Appleby won't know about that, sir, but I expect you remember it clearly enough.'

'Certainly I do.'

'All sorts of odd ideas were going through my head. For instance, there was this Ibell and his bloody gun. Sorry, Lady Appleby – this Ibell and his gun. He struck me as having turned up pat. Or had *we* turned up on *him* pat? I mean, was it a regular turn of his, so that he was as predictable as a copper on his beat?'

'Coppers are no longer predictable on their beat. After about a century of predictability, you see, it dawned on us that unpredictability might be a little more effective in the war against crime. But continue.'

'And then there was the odd business of Bobby being hauled in to have a word with old Mr Ashmore. And the other odd business of spying on him. I think I told you about that, sir. I started it, as a matter of fact. Bobby thought it wasn't on, and he was quite right. Which makes it queer that I found myself wanting to do it all over again. I went back to the terrace. It was a damned silly thing to do' – Finn paused here, as if determining whether this expression required a further apology to Lady Appleby – 'really too damned silly, for there was quite a lot of moonlight tumbling around again, and the chap with his gun might appear and have a further go at any time. For a moment I thought it *was* the chap. I was scared stiff.'

'You thought *who* was the chap?' Not unnaturally, Judith was perplexed.

'This chap at the front door. I think I got round to

telling Sir John about him last night. But he didn't have a gun, and for a moment I had a queer impression it was Giles. Then I saw he was quite old. I couldn't make out what he was doing. At first I thought he must be trying to pick the lock. I stopped — and again it was pretty silly, since I'd be in full view the second he turned round. But at least I tumbled to what he was up to. He was polishing the door-bell. And then — just in the second that I stood there — he finished up on the bell and started in on the door-handle. Did you ever hear of anything so crazy? An elderly man putting on this housemaid's turn by moonlight.'

'Most remarkable,' Appleby said. 'Do you happen to be able to tell us whether he had all the usual stuff to hand? A tin of polish, for example, or the kind of soft brush sometimes used on the job?'

'I don't know. All I actually saw was a cloth. It might have been a big coloured handkerchief.'

'I have little doubt that it was a big coloured handkerchief.' For the first time in this curious conversation — it seemed to Judith — her husband had spoken with a gravity that was wholly without irony. 'And then you had — as I rather gathered — your not altogether fortunate encounter with him?'

'That's right, sir.' Rather surprisingly, Finn had faintly flushed. 'It's really rather embarrassing. And it's *not* as if I'd been tight. And he was quite an old man. I *am* certain of that.' Finn turned to Judith. 'About Sir John's age, I'd say, Lady Appleby.'

'Or mine?' Lady Appleby appeared impressed. 'I'm surprised that he retained the bodily vigour even to polish up the handle of the big front door.'

'Oh, I say!' Finn appeared to be aware of having occasioned amusement. 'I mean, you know, that it shouldn't have been an equal contest. I ought to have been right on top from the start. As a matter of fact, that's why I *did* start.'

'Do you mean, Finn' — Judith had decided that whether

Finn was Something Finn or Finn Something he could no longer with civility be denied a name – 'do you mean that you started a fight with this person?'

'Yes, Lady Appleby, just that. By the way, I'm Cedric Finn. But Cedric is so awfully silly that I like everybody to call me just Finn. I'm so glad you're going to. Yes – I thought I ought to grab the chap. And perhaps shout for Mr Ashmore, or even for Ibell. He was plainly a lunatic, you see. Only a lunatic would go round polishing brass by moonlight. The moonlight might be significant, don't you think? Lunatics and moonlight have something to do with each other. I can never remember just what.'

'And what happened then, Finn?' Judith tried to put this question – to which the answer was already painfully obvious – as kindly as possible.

'He just knocked me out. Square on the jaw, you know. It was as simple as that. And that's why there's hardly a bruise to show. The jaw just goes back *click*, you see, and hits something, and there you are. Of course, there is the fact that he was a maniac. Maniacs are always frightfully strong. I've read that somewhere. Have you?'

'It is at least a common persuasion,' Appleby said. 'And the man's conduct certainly suggests an imperfectly balanced mind. But had you any other reason to question his sanity?'

'He *looked* mad. Incredibly ferocious.'

'Eventually you must have come to your senses – or perhaps I ought to say have recovered consciousness. For here, after all, you are. Will you have another cup of coffee?'

'Oh, yes – please. Black will be splendid. I don't terribly care for milk. Hot and in coffee, I mean. It was awfully good of you, sir, to find me that milk last night.'

'Just what did happen when you recovered from this brutal assault?'

'The chap had disappeared. I was rather relieved about that. He might have been standing over me, prepared to slosh me again. I got up and rubbed my jaw. And then I thought I shouldn't be put off.

'By this vexatious interruption?'

'Just that, sir. I decided to go on having that look around – even if this maniac, and Ibell as well, were still about the place.'

'Don't you think,' Judith asked, 'that the maniac and Ibell may have been one and the same man?'

'Well, no – not really.' Finn considered. 'I had a strong impression that the maniac was a gent.'

'One always knows,' Appleby asked gravely, 'when it is a gentleman who has knocked one out?'

'Not exactly that.' Finn looked at his host with a kind of reproachful suspicion. 'It was the clothes, and all that. There was this moonlight around, remember.'

'You would recognize the maniac again?'

'Oh, yes – I'm sure I should. Well, I dusted myself down, and moved along the terrace. There was still that lighted window – the one we'd been doing the spying at. But when I got to it I found it was no go, so far as seeing into the room went. There had been a small gap in the curtains before, you see. But now they were drawn close. After that, I got a funny idea in my head.' Finn hesitated. 'It's really so silly that I hardly like to mention it. Particularly to you, sir, since they're your sort of thing.'

'Just what are you thinking of as being my sort of thing?'

'Fingerprints.'

'You got round to thinking about fingerprints?' Appleby was looking at Finn in considerable astonishment. 'On the door-handle and the door-bell?'

'It just came into my head, as I say.' Finn sounded extremely apologetic. 'The maniac had rung the bell and turned the handle. And when I saw him he was removing any telltale marks. Awful nonsense, of course. I must have been reading too many thrillers.'

'Might this man have come out of the house?'

'Well, that's the next thing I have to tell you. The last thing, really. I decided I'd try to make sure that Mr Ashmore was all right. The fact that there was a light on still in that downstairs room suggested he hadn't started going to bed. So I decided I'd ring the bell myself, and just say hullo to him.'

'As he has never set eyes on you, he might have been mildly surprised. But your plan didn't come off?'

'No, sir. I rang twice, and nothing happened. So I felt a bit of a fool. I had a notion Mr Ashmore lives all alone in the place, and it struck me there might be an hour after which he just didn't care to open his door. So I gave up, and came away. It took me a terribly long time to get back to Dream. I did a kind of Snakes-and-Ladders hitch-hiking.'

'Did you, by any chance, try that door-handle?'

'Well, yes – I did. It sounds awful cheek, and if the door had turned out to be unlocked I don't think I'd have had the nerve to walk in. But I did try it.'

'Could the maniac have come out of the house and locked the door behind him?'

'He could have, in a way. It's a Yale lock. He could have shoved up the little button thing inside as he came out, and then it would have locked itself automatically.'

'I see.' Remarking that Finn had now concluded a substantial repast, Appleby pushed forward a cigarette-box. 'There's one thing I'd like to ask you more particularly about this man you came upon at the door. And we'll stop, for the moment, calling him the maniac. You say he looked ferocious. Are you speaking of what had the appearance of a settled disposition, or of features momentarily contorted by anger or fury?'

'Oh, I say!' For a second it looked as if this discrimination was beyond Finn's powers to reflect on. But this proved not to be the case. 'Well, sir, I don't think he'd ever look a terribly nice person. But there was quite a lot just happening on his face in the very short time I had my dekko at it. At bay – that sort of thing.'

'Rage?'

'Rage, all right.'

'Surprise?'

'Surprise, certainly.'

'Terror?'

'I think I'd rather say fear, sir.' Finn paused, as if rather astonished by this nicety. 'He was scared, all right – which was why he hit out quick, I suppose.'

'I wonder whether –'

Appleby paused, for the breakfast-room door had opened, and Mrs Colpoys stood framed in it.

'Colonel Pride is on the telephone, sir. And he says it's urgent.'

14

Bobby Appleby came downstairs half an hour later, and made his way hopefully to the kitchen. Mrs Colpoys was polishing silver.

'If you want coffee, Mr Robert, you must make it for yourself. A busy woman can't be expected to run a cafeteria service. But at least the milk has come.'

'All right, Mrs C. Do you mind if I get busy on the grill as well?'

'Well, don't make a mess.' Mrs Colpoys rubbed vigorously. 'There's plenty of bacon, but don't touch those kidneys. They're for a *sauté* tonight. If you look in the brown bowl you'll find some particularly large eggs.'

'You spoil me, you splendid woman.' Bobby moved contentedly about the kitchen. 'I say, Mrs. C., do you happen to know whether my friend came in last night?'

'Of course he came in. He'd be no gentleman if he hadn't. There are limits to the ways college boys can carry on.'

'We're not college boys any longer, Mrs C.'

'Perhaps not – but it's the behaviour that counts.' Mrs Colpoys shook her silver-polish vigorously. 'Your friend came in at I don't know what hour in the morning. And disturbed your father, it seems. Your father poured a pint of milk into him, and then had to listen to I don't know what nonsense. Not that your friend sounded as if he were drunk. I won't say that of him. But so excited that your father had to put him to bed. He might have got you up to do that for him I'd have thought, Mr Robert. Not that you came home at a very early hour yourself. I heard you. And her ladyship's light didn't go out until she heard you safely in the house. But she won't have let on to Sir John about that.'

'Mrs C., you're a very observing woman. I had to see somebody off on a train at Linger Junction.'

'Well, I've no doubt an escort must do his duty.' Mrs Colpoys sounded mollified. 'I'm glad to know it was at least a lady, and not one of those young trollops from the village.'

'You have a shocking old mind, Mrs C. It comes of a lifetime in good service. As a matter of fact, I haven't spoken either to a trollop or a young gentlewoman for weeks.'

'I don't call that anything to be proud of.' As she achieved this volte-face, Mrs Colpoys picked up a Georgian cream-jug. 'Not wholesome, at all. And now you come gossiping, and keeping an old woman from her work. Now, stop it, Mr Robert.' Mrs Colpoys flushed with artless pleasure as Bobby kissed her. 'Here I am, behind-hand already, and not even knowing whether your father will be home to lunch.'

'He's gone out?'

'Appealed to by that Colonel Pride. The Chief Constable.' Mrs Colpoys made this communication with great satisfaction. 'Urgent, the Colonel said it was. Sir John is a long-suffering man. Hurried away, he has, and taken your precious friend with him.'

'Taken Finn?' Bobby put down his knife and fork in astonishment. 'Taken Finn to see the Chief Constable?'

'That he has. And left a message for you with her lady-ship. If you've finished eating me out of my kitchen you'd better be off and find her.'

Bobby did as he was told, and came upon his mother arranging a bowl of chrysanthemums in the hall. He wondered why she was putting in time in this ladylike way instead of slapping clay around in her studio. Then he saw that she had the rather still expression she wore when something disturbing or unfortunate had happened.

'Mummy, what on earth is this about Daddy and Finn and Colonel Pride?'

'Have you had breakfast?'

'Yes.'

'Tommy Pride rang up to tell your father that Martyn Ashmore is dead. Tommy just heard.'

'That old man dead!' Bobby looked blankly at his mother. 'I'm very sorry to hear it. But why on earth should Pride have heard about it so soon – and want to get hold of Daddy?'

'It ties up with other things, I suppose. Including the nonsense that you and those two young men were up to last night. I gather you actually did go to the Chase?'

'Yes, we did.'

'It seems to have been rather a dangerous place recently. Your father was very nearly killed there the other day. Has he told you?'

'Good God! No, he hasn't. You mean in some accident?'

'It didn't seem very like an accident. Equally, it might have been Martyn Ashmore who was killed ... then.'

'Daddy ought to have told me – I mean, when he knew we were going to be fooling around there.'

'I rather agree with you.' Lady Appleby was extremely calm. 'But you must remember how much such things have been part of the day's work with him all his life.'

'Yes, of course.' Bobby was surprised to find himself feeling rather sick. 'Do you mean that the old man has been *killed*?'

'Killed? Murdered? I'm not the police, and I can't tell you. They can't tell themselves, for that matter. Your father has gone off with his fingers crossed.'

'Mummy – what do you mean?'

'He told Tommy at once about what you three had been up to. Tommy was very nice. He said instantly he had some hope that it would turn out to have been a C.V.A.'

'What on earth is that?'

'It's doctors' and coroners' shorthand for cerebro-vascular accident.' Lady Appleby smiled faintly. 'And that's just technical jargon for a stroke.'

'I see,' Bobby said slowly. 'I was taken in, you know.'

'Taken in? Hoodwinked?'

'No, no – I don't mean that. Taken into the Chase by his nephew – Finn's friend Giles. I talked to him. He seemed quite all right.'

'But odd things were happening?'

'I suppose one would have to say that. Ashmore and Giles had a talk about that beastly girl. It seems that the old man himself –'

'Yes, I know.'

'So there was that – shabby deceptions with the makings of something nasty in them, I suppose. And, for good measure, there was a demented keeper with a gun.'

'I've heard that too, Bobby. And your friend Finn – he continued to hang around, you see – ran into something odder still. It's my guess that a great many inquiries will have to be made. And that brings me to your father's message. You know where King's Yatter is?'

'Yes, of course.'

'You are to go straight there now, get hold of Giles Ashmore again quite quietly, and take him over to the Chase. Daddy will be there – as a policeman more or less, you should remember – and so will the Chief Constable and his surgeon and a whole crime squad. I'm sorry.'

'Mummy, it won't get me down – not even if I'm to be painfully exhibited as having been fooling around like a kid. Will Daddy think it awful?'

'No, he will not. Of course, he will like it better if you show some brains. I expect you will.'

'Thanks a lot. But, by the way, I don't know about Giles. If I can get hold of him, I mean. It's quite likely he won't be back yet. But I'm forgetting I haven't told you. I shoved him on the midnight train for London. He was determined to see the girl. Quite right, in a way.'

'I suppose so.' With an effect of some concentration,

Lady Appleby stepped back to examine the effect of her flowers. 'Whatever has happened,' she said, 'there is bound to be an inquest. Not all the doctors in the county, with the Lord Lieutenant himself behind them, could prevent that. In fact there's a disgusting scandal ahead.' Lady Appleby stepped forward again, and altered the position of the chrysanthemums in relation to the dark panelling behind them. She gave a nod of satisfaction. 'Never mind,' she said briskly to her son. 'And now be off.'

'Even if I don't find Giles, I still go on to the Chase?'

'Yes, of course. Don't waste time.' Lady Appleby smiled suddenly. 'Only don't drive that ancient thing *too* fast. Remember there will be coppers all over the place.' She put down a pair of scissors. 'Hoobin's cocoa,' she said. 'That's the next thing.'

15

There was no Appleby or Raven fortune to speak of, and neither Bobby Appleby nor his brother and sisters had much thought of anything that could be called a patrimony. Probably Dream would have to be sold up one day, and that would be that. This situation had one consequence at the moment: Bobby had driven half-way to King's Yatter before it came into his head that numerous Ashmores must have fresh expectations as a result of Martyn Ashmore's death. Rupert Ashmore, father of Giles and of de Voisin's fiancée Virginia, was probably the person most immediately affected. Unless Bobby had got things wrong, Rupert was now the head of the family, and would be due to inherit the Chase. But Martyn Ashmore had at least enjoyed the reputation of being very wealthy, and if this was true there would be a lot more going. Of course the dead man had notoriously disliked his relations (doubtless including the wretched Giles, whom he had been amusing himself by making a fool of), and this might mean that he would leave all the wealth he could to, say, an Oxford college or a home for stray dogs. But Bobby had a notion that this was something which didn't often really happen. Even detested relations usually came in for their whack.

It was a sunny morning with a nip in the air, and as he crossed the downs at a good pace once more Bobby's spirits rose. The notion that on the previous night the Chase had really seen some deed of dreadful note was surely extravagant. There wasn't all that to be said for the country gentry; he seldom found them other than dismally dull; but at least it wasn't their habit to go in for crimes of violence. His father probably found them dismally dull too – and perhaps for precisely this reason. That was it. His father, in too placid and uneventful a retirement, was taking to fancying things. Bobby shoved the accelerator farther down. He felt a little sorry for his father. As for his mother, she was easily upset. She didn't at all want crime bobbing up in the vicinity; as John Appleby's wife she had come in for quite enough of it. But by now she would have taken Hoobin his cocoa and gone off to mess about with her clay. That was clearly one of the pleasant things about a career in the plastic arts. You could keep it up pretty well to the grave. Since it was all a matter of exploring formal relations it didn't really require – as writing, on the other hand, did – any constant access of fresh human experience.

Bobby Appleby began to whistle as he drove – and then checked himself, feeling that perhaps it wasn't quite decent. It struck him that it was a bit feeble to be hoping that any real excitement over Martyn Ashmore's death would fade out. What was involvement (in not too desperately intimate a relation) with crime and guilt and misery except very much an access of fresh human experience? Bobby assumed a more serious expression, waited for a signpost that said 'King's Yatter 12, Abbot's Yatter 4', and turned off the high road.

The house was a half-timber affair with a thatched roof; there was plenty of it, but it was probably more picturesque than comfortable. At the back there was a large garden, walled round in ancient brick. There didn't seem to be more land than that. Bobby wondered whether Rupert Ashmore did, or had ever done, anything in particular. He wasn't a Colonel or a Commander or an Honourable, like so many people living in this sort of style round these parts. A City gent, perhaps. Or just a gent.

Bobby remembered that his instructions were to get hold of Giles Ashmore 'quite quietly'. He was sure that these had been his mother's words, and they suddenly struck him as a little odd. Rupert Ashmore was presumably the next proprietor of the Chase, and he was quite certainly what was called the dead man's next of kin. Surely he would have been told by this time of his brother's death? It seemed impossible that even Colonel Pride could take the responsibility of keeping him in the dark about it for more than an hour or two. Perhaps Rupert was known to be away from home. That might be it.

Giles – as Bobby had now worked it out – would undoubtedly still be absent. He couldn't even have changed his mind about London, for the train into which Bobby had shoved him, and which he had watched leave the Junction, travelled non-stop to Paddington. Even if Giles had lost his nerve there – which was likely enough – he could hardly have turned tail and got home by now. Bobby wondered whether there was a Mrs Rupert. He had a notion that Rupert himself was almost as old as Martyn. That meant well past the span allotted to us by the Psalmist. But then the Psalmist was almost gruesomely out of date. (Gruesomely, Bobby added to himself, except when one is thinking of one's parents, old housemaster, former tutor, and a few other persons to be viewed in a sentimental light.) People – or at least people who inhabited houses like King's Yatter – now invariably lived to an enormous age. Even if they were Ashmores only by marriage they did that. So in all probability there was a Mrs Rupert. Perhaps it would be Mrs Rupert – silver-haired, gracious, and rather puzzled – who would receive him when he asked for Giles. He would have to fish around to discover whether she had received the distressing news about her disagreeable brother-in-law. If she hadn't, he would have to decide whether he was meant to tell her. And he hadn't been given a clue. Perhaps his father designed that he should use those brains. Bobby himself had never been sure that he *had* brains. He had once been possessed of a sort of rapid cunning useful on a

Rugger-field. But his writing didn't seem to have much to do with brains. It was something that bobbed up in his head – he really didn't at all know how. It wasn't even part of what could be called his normal personality – the personality, for example, or the chap who went around with chaps like Giles and Finn.

Bobby Appleby (it will be observed) had fallen as he drove upon an absorbingly interesting subject. This was why he had to brake rather sharply in order not to kill somebody.

It was a girl – surrounded by dachshunds of the long-haired sort, and behaving as if she and they owned the road. This, indeed, might well be the state of the case, since he was now on the very short drive leading up to Mr Rupert Ashmore's residence.

'I'm most frightfully sorry,' Bobby said. At least – since the Mercedes was an open car – he didn't have to stick his head in an idiotic manner through a window. Before looking at the girl he had looked at her nasty little dogs, since he felt that it was solicitude in that direction which would go down well. 'I hope I didn't startle them.' He transferred his gaze, and as a result was uncommonly startled himself. She was an overwhelmingly beautiful girl. The overwhelmingness was perhaps a consequence of that celibate life which Bobby – as he had lately informed Mrs Colpoys – had been maintaining for weeks. It was striking, all the same.

'We weren't startled, at all,' the girl said politely. Very vexatiously, she gave no sign of being immediately pre-possessed by Robert Appleby (Rugger Blue, promising anti-novelist). 'Have you lost your way?'

'Well, no – I don't think so. I'm looking for a friend I believe lives here. Giles Ashmore.'

'I'm Giles's sister, Virgina. You must be Finn.'

'I'm not Finn. My name is Appleby. Bobby. I haven't known Giles for very long.'

'How do you do? I'm afraid Giles is away. That's to say,

he went off yesterday, and hasn't come back yet. I don't know why. He isn't at all wild.'

'I suppose not.' It had just dawned on Bobby – to an effect of somewhat absurd dismay – that this girl was engaged to the young Frenchman he had stumbled upon on the previous evening. It seemed a most unnecessary entanglement. Bobby felt rather cross. This made him speak abruptly. 'As a matter of fact,' he said, 'Giles has gone off in a hurry to see Robina.'

'Oh.' Miss Ashmore put something decidedly chilly into this monosyllable.

'Is either of your parents at home?' Bobby had remembered that there *was* a Mrs Rupert. She had accepted Robina sufficiently to tote her round. Hence the plebeian girl's fatal *rencontre* with the late Martyn Ashmore. Socially regarded, Mrs Rupert must be more open-minded than her daughter.

'My mother is at home. My father went to London yesterday afternoon.'

'I don't suppose *he* went to see this Robina Bunker, by any chance?'

'I hardly suppose so.' Virginia Ashmore said this very coldly indeed. 'My father does not wholly approve of my brother's engagement. It is kind of you to be so interested in us, Mr Appleby. Are you the police officer's son?'

'Yes, I am.' Bobby felt angry. 'Police officer' contrived to be both accurate and derogatory.

'So your father is a Bobby too.' Miss Ashmore produced this impertinent joke as if it were a substantial witticism. 'Should you care to see my mother?'

'I don't think so, thank you.' Bobby, although he had decided to hate Virginia Ashmore, hesitated for a moment. Regarded merely as a visual object, she was so compelling that he almost felt prepared to stand and be insulted by her indefinitely. Were one to venture to imagine her as a tactile sensation – Bobby pulled himself together. 'I had the pleasure of meeting Monsieur de Voisin last night,' he said with some formality.

'Jules?' Miss Ashmore appeared startled. 'Where was that?'

'Near the Chase. He had been visiting your uncle. Isn't he staying here?'

'Yes – for a few days longer. He didn't mention going to the Chase, although it is natural enough, of course, that he should visit my uncle.'

'All you Ashmores are a bit at odds with each other, aren't you?'

If Rupert Ashmore's daughter thought this an outrageous remark she refrained from saying so. But she did summon her dachshunds around her, as if proposing to conclude the encounter.

'Can I give my brother a message?' she asked.

'That's very good of you.' Bobby now felt extremely awkward. It didn't seem reasonable to go away without telling this girl – however little he had determined to fancy her – what had happened to her uncle. 'As a matter of fact,' he said, 'I had bad news for him – which I think none of you can have heard. It's about Mr Martyn Ashmore.'

'Uncle Martyn? Has he done something hopelessly embarrassing?'

'I hope it needn't be called that. He has died – rather suddenly.'

'Oh!' Miss Ashmore had turned pale. 'How dreadful! I hardly ever saw him. He was mad.'

'If you hardly ever saw him, how can you know that?'

'Mr Appleby, your manner is extremely strange. My uncle's state was well known. My father has explained it to me. Martyn Ashmore suffered from paranoia. He had delusions of persecution. It was becoming apparent that something must be done about it.'

'Well, nothing need be done about it now.' Bobby glanced curiously at the girl. It was *her* manner that was extremely strange; she had spoken ironically and as if by rote. 'Will you tell your brother, when he gets home? And your mother and fiancé, I suppose. The police will probably be trying to contact your father.'

'The police!' As if she felt not too steady on her shapely limbs, Miss Ashmore took hold of the door of Bobby's car. 'Is it something dreadful? Did my uncle kill himself?'

'I'm terribly sorry, Miss Ashmore. I don't really know much about it. But I don't think there is any suspicion of just that.'

'Not through ... fear?'

'Fear?' Bobby was puzzled. 'I suppose fear – of disease, perhaps, or even of persecution – makes people take their own lives sometimes. I hope it's been nothing of the kind. As a matter of fact, I'm on my way to the Chase now. I was to fetch Giles there. My father has gone over. The Chief Constable asked him to.' Bobby had decided to be wholly frank. 'Shall I bring back any news to you?'

'Take me there – at once.'

'But ought you not, perhaps, to tell your mother?' Bobby was almost alarmed.

'At once, please.' Virginia Ashmore had actually opened the door of the car.

'But what about the dogs?' This was a perfectly sensible question, but Bobby somehow felt idiotic as he asked it. 'Shall we,' he went on more resourcefully, 'put them in the back?'

'They'll go home. They don't like cars.' Bobby found that the girl was sitting beside him. 'I suppose you know,' she said, 'about strange things that have been going on?'

'Well, yes – I know about some. I think my father knows about rather more.'

'So does mine, Mr Appleby.'

Bobby said nothing. For good or ill, he had a passenger, and he concentrated on turning the long Mercedes in the narrow drive. He was conscious of wanting to make a neat job of it. For a moment it looked as if the beastly little dogs were going to be a complication. But they gathered into a small pack and made off towards the house –

plainly disapproving of the whole thing. It was only when he was out on the road that Bobby spoke.

'And your brother?' he asked.

'Giles is by himself.'

'I know – if he hasn't joined Miss Bunker.'

'I don't mean that. I mean that Giles walks by himself, like Kipling's cat.'

'He doesn't muck in?' It seemed to Bobby that Virginia Ashmore had made her first civilized remark. 'Not with the rest of the family?'

'Just that. Uncle Martyn was supposed to be frightening. But it's Giles who frightens me.'

'And Monsieur de Voisin – Jules?'

'Jules has been very angry. The French are not scrupulous. But they detest the bizarre.'

'I see.' Bobby said this automatically, for in fact he felt in very considerable darkness. But it struck him that Virginia was by no means as dumb – in the slang sense – as very beautiful girls so often and so disappointingly were. 'I think I ought to tell you that there is probably a whole *posse* of police at the Chase.'

'Naturally, if what you are hinting at is true.'

'I've no business to hint anything.' Bobby suddenly felt very bad. 'And there's something else I must say. I was at the Chase last night myself. Along with your brother and my crackpot friend Finn. And we were being damnably silly.'

'Where is Finn now?'

'At the Chase. My father took him there. I haven't seen him since – well, since the middle of things last night. There was a kind of row. He told Giles and me to sod off, more or less.' Bobby's use of this expression rather surprised him. It admitted Virginia into a kind of intimacy. He and his friends employed the idiom of their simpler contemporaries only among themselves. 'And listen,' he said. 'I believe Colonel Pride – that's the Chief Constable, who's a friend of my family – is a very decent chap. Still – talk to my father, if you want to talk.'

'Bobby Senior?' For the first time in this strange encounter, Miss Ashmore faintly smiled. 'I apologize for that crack.'

'Not a bit,' Bobby said. He was wondering how his father would react when, having failed to turn up with the aspiring curator of museums, he turned up with this show-piece of a girl instead. 'You don't think,' he asked, 'that we ought to go back and fetch Jules too?'

'Why should we do that?'

This question curiously discomposed Bobby – so much so, that he failed to find a reply.

'Jules can look after the dogs,' Virginia said. 'He gave them to me.'

'Really? They're terribly jolly.'

'Don't be silly.'

Bobby's head swam. This girl was getting at him badly. He saw with a horrid clearness that she was going to cause him sleepless nights.

'Was it you who wrote *The Lumber Room*?' Virginia asked suddenly.

'Yes, it was.' Bobby positively clutched at the wheel of his car.

'I thought it – well, terribly jolly.'

'You are a devil,' Bobby said.

'No, I'm not.' The girl beside Bobby Appleby spoke in a changed voice. 'But I think there may be a devil around.'

Part Five

Abbot's Yatter and Elsewhere

16

The body had been removed, but not the blood from the hearthstone. Hearthstone and threshold, Appleby thought: blood found on these cries out louder than any other. Cries out, that is to say, in the remote recesses of the mind. But there are other symbolic places too. Odour of blood on the ancestral stair. Yeats.

A wounded scalp bleeds freely, even if the wound has caused almost instant death. There was quite a lot of blood. Small splashes, which had congealed soonest, were now curling up at the edges. These might at any moment take flight, one could feel, like the autumn leaves in the park outside – but upwards to some supernal judgement seat to cry for vengeance. There had been one deeper pool, and some downward draught from the great chimney had puffed wood-ash into it from the extinguished fire. The effect was of some small fur-clad creature, mangled and flattened by a passing wheel.

'The electric light was still on,' Colonel Pride said. 'I call that a sign that tells against foul play.'

'Why?' Appleby asked, and looked about him. This was not a room into which the dead man had taken him on that curious morning. The reason was perhaps that there were no portraits in it. But it was well furnished and there were various signs of a willingness to enjoy rational comfort: the fire had been a large one; books and papers were scattered around; on a side-table there was quite an array of bottles. Appleby strolled over and inspected the bottles. What he didn't expect to see – sure enough – he didn't see. He turned back to Pride. 'But why?' he repeated curiously.

'Think of having killed a man in a lighted room like this. What would it be your instinct to do as you cleared out? Switch off the light.'

'I see. Only heaven can peep through the blanket of the dark.'

'And cry "Hold, hold!",' Finn said unexpectedly.

'Too late to cry that when the brains are already out,' Appleby murmured. He had walked to the window and was gazing at the terrace. 'And they pretty well were out?' he asked, without turning round. 'I suppose I'd better go and look. But that was the state of the case?'

'Yes – and it's what worries my surgeon.' Pride looked doubtfully at Finn; it wasn't very clear to him why the young man should be there. 'His first conviction was that there must have been a blow; that no simple fall could produce such damage. But he seems to have shifted ground now, and to be having doubts. Or say making reservations. He doesn't want to be too positive one way or the other, if you ask me, until some chap much higher up in all that forensic stuff has given an opinion. I've asked for a real swell to be sent from town.'

'Very wise.' Appleby turned back into the room, nodding absently. 'It's a fact that these things can be very tricky. And various aspects of them can be pretty easily faked.'

'My sawbones says that too.' Pride pointed to the fireplace. 'That big firedog on the left – the one tilted over, but with the charred log still resting on it. There was blood and hair on it. They were almost certainly –' Pride hesitated. 'Almost certainly his. Of course, there have to be tests. But my chap says that *they* could be faked. Or, alternatively, that they are the product of a fortuitous accident-like sequel to a deliberate and lethal assault.'

'Always alternatives,' Appleby said. 'Lots of them. Common form. People fall with a very varying velocity, you know. And with very varying results. Their weight can be a factor. And sudden spasm of one sort or another. As for results – well, bones differ, skulls differ, old age takes one body one way and another quite another. How many expert witnesses have I heard debating such things in my time.'

'No doubt, my dear – um – John.' Colonel Pride appeared not to find this reminiscent note useful. 'My fellow says all that. He also says one ought to begin by simply considering the most obvious and most natural thing.'

'Quite right – and that's what we'll do. And – do you know? – we'll ask Finn. The unprofessional angle is often the most productive. Finn, what is the obvious and most natural explanation of this unfortunate affair?'

'I've been thinking, sir.' Finn was less startled by Appleby's sudden appeal than might have been expected. 'When we did that Peeping Tom stuff –'

'Can't understand that,' Pride interrupted gruffly. 'Behaviour of mere louts. Most unaccountable.'

'Yes, sir.' Finn, properly humble, directed a cautious grin at Appleby. 'But there we were; and there was Mr Martyn Ashmore, comfortably settled with a book – and rather close to what looked like rather a warm fire. He must have got up and had one prowl around, I'd say, because he seems to have noticed that the curtains were not properly drawn, and to have put that right. I think he probably went on reading for quite a time before anything happened –'

'Not much doubt about that.' Colonel Pride had interrupted again, and this time it was impatiently. 'Whatever happened, the result was his pitching head and shoulders into that fireplace. But he wasn't burnt or even singed. Fire must have been pretty well out. Hours after your last sight of him. Young man, go on.'

'Well, sir. I'd say the room got a bit hot, and he simply fell asleep. Deep sleep and perhaps – as you say – for hours. Then he started awake and got confused, as old people are said to do. I expect, sir, you know the sensation.'

'I know nothing of the sort.' Pride spoke with some asperity. 'Continue.'

'That's about it. The poor old chap jumped up, stumbled, and went down with a crash. And that firedog thing cracked his head open. That's the obvious explanation.'

'Do you believe it?'

'I don't think that's material, sir.' Finn said this with some dignity. 'I'm not an expert on smashed skulls or the – the physiology of senescence.'

'I suppose not. But you were around this house last night when you had no business to be –'

'I can't quite agree to that, sir.' Finn was unexpectedly firm. 'We were led into something a bit silly. But we had a perfectly proper occasion for calling on Mr Ashmore.'

'Quite right,' Appleby said. 'Don't forget, Tommy, that my own boy was in on it. And Bobby would certainly not lend himself to any impropriety. Reflect on your knowledge of his mother's character, my dear chap.'

'Quite so, quite so.' Somewhat to Appleby's surprise, Tommy Pride allowed himself to be cautiously amused. 'But Mr Finn has this uncommonly odd story about somebody knocking him down. Mark you, I accept it. The other story – the one about the fellow with the gun – seemed a pretty tall yarn to me. But, of course, it has been substantiated. The keeper Ibell admits to having fired the thing several times. A matter of warning shots, he says. Most improper, to my mind. Still, he behaved quite sensibly when he found the body.'

'I haven't gathered how he came to do that,' Appleby said.

'It seems that nobody except Ashmore has been sleeping in the house, and that Ibell has had the job of giving him a call at eight o'clock. Literally a call. Not coming into the house, but simply bellowing up at his window.'

'Is that a usual sort of thing?' Finn asked innocently. 'I mean, among the rural gentry?'

'Of course it is nothing of the kind, sir.' Pride looked severely at Finn. 'Mr Ashmore was plainly a most eccentric character. Just how eccentric, we perhaps don't yet know. Well, Ibell failed this morning to get any response from his employer, and when he saw that there was still a light on in this room, he became alarmed, and entered.'

'Entered?' Appleby repeated. 'Although he wasn't allowed to come in and rouse Ashmore in a reasonable manner, he nevertheless had a key?'

'Apparently not. He says that Ashmore believed he went round locking up everything at night, but never quite managed to complete the job. You could always find a way in, if you wanted to.'

'I wonder whether many people knew that?'

'I don't see why they should.'

'I bet I could have got in last night, if I'd wanted to,' Finn said cheerfully. 'A pity, really, that I didn't do a little lawbreaking in a serious way.'

'Mr Finn, I don't advise you to cultivate that attitude of mind,' Pride said. His disapproval of this young man appeared to be mounting. 'And I don't know that you can be of further help to us at the moment.'

'I don't at all object to getting out of this,' Finn said. 'I'll take a walk in the park until Sir John's ready for me.'

'Just a moment, Finn.' Appleby had picked up his hat. 'I'd rather you didn't. As a matter of fact, I don't intend to let you out of my sight.'

'Oh, I say!' Not surprisingly, Finn was indignant and alarmed. 'Do you mean I'm being suspected of something?'

'I mean no more than that you and I will go for a short run. If you will be so good, that's to say. Only a matter of making a call somewhere.' Appleby turned to Pride 'I expect Bobby over a little later in the morning,' he said. 'And with a companion, I rather hope. But Finn and I may be back by then.'

'I'd rather hoped we might – um – confer,' Pride said. He spoke a shade stiffly, and with a further glare at Finn.

'I think that, by lunch time, we may have rather more to confer about.'

'Do you really think so?' Colonel Pride brightened

visibly. 'I'm bound to say I'd like to get this wretched affair cleared up quietly.'

'I can't promise quiet,' Appleby said, and motioned Finn out of the room.

'And the first thing is a telephone,' Appleby said, as he climbed into his car. 'Do you know that Martyn Ashmore's line was cut off because he refused to pay what he said were exorbitant bills from the Postmaster-General? I don't know how Pride's coppers are getting along. Probably they have some sort of wireless.'

'Probably,' Finn said politely, and reflected that Bobby's father didn't sound quite with it in modern techniques of fighting crime. He'd let things slip rather, no doubt, since he retired. 'There's an A. A. telephone a quarter of a mile along the main road,' he added helpfully. 'I noticed it last night.'

'Then we'll make for that – before paying this social call.' Appleby smiled benignly. 'One mustn't let a disturbance like this, you know, interfere with neighbourly duty.'

'I suppose not.' It suddenly struck Finn that old Appleby was actually a bit gaga. This perception embarrassed him, and he remained silent until after the telephone call had been completed.

'I rang up my wife,' Appleby said, as he slipped into gear again. 'Bobby's on his way over, but it won't be after having collected Giles Ashmore. It seems that Giles departed for London on the midnight train.'

'He's bolted – Giles?'

'Bolted?' Appleby glanced curiously at Finn. 'I suppose it could be called that. But the ostensible object of the exercise was to reproach the faithless Robina.' Appleby paused. 'What puts the idea of bolting in your head, Finn?'

'Nothing sensible, sir, I suppose. Giles can't have done in his uncle. That train was non-stop to Paddington. Or could he have pulled the communcation-cord somewhere beyond Linger?'

'My dear young man, do you really think that Giles Ashmore could murder somebody – any more than you could yourself?'

'Oh, I don't know about that. About myself, that is.' Finn seemed rather offended at being taxed with too much of the milk of human kindness for effective homicidal action. 'And one gets to suspecting everybody all round, it seems to me, when a thing like this happens.'

'But you put to the Chief Constable quite a persuasive case for viewing Ashmore's death as an accident.'

'I refused to say I believed it.' Finn spoke quite sharply. 'Where are we going now, sir?'

'To Abbot's Yatter. You are going to ask if Mr Giles is at home.'

'You've got it wrong, Sir John.' Finn's view of the twilight character of Appleby's intellectual processes was confirmed. 'King's Yatter is Giles's home – not Abbot's Yatter.'

'So it is, Finn. Nevertheless, I hope you will do as I suggest. Rather noisily, insistently, and obtusely, if possible. Do you think you could manage an effect of being obtuse?'

'Oh, I say!'

'Abbott's Yatter is, of course, Ambrose Ashmore's house. You've never been there?'

'Never been near the place.'

'And they won't know anything about you – for example, that you realize there are two Yatters?'

'I don't think so. I gather from old Giles that not much information passes between the two Yatters. All the Ashmores detest each other, it seems. That's what makes this such a funny business, wouldn't you say, sir?'

'Absolutely hilarious. Take this key' – Appleby had contrived to reach into a waistcoat-pocket – 'and unlock the glove-box. Fetch out what you find there.'

'Oh, I say!' For the second time within a couple of

minutes, Finn was constrained to his prime conversational resource in moments of stress. 'Is it loaded?'

'Most certainly it is. Don't touch the safety-catch.'

'Am I to take it with me, sir?'

'Heaven forbid. It is strictly for my personal use. I think we'll make a detour here. No point in running into Bobby, and having to waste time stopping and explaining ourselves.'

'But if you want to be up to something rather deep at Abbot's Yatter, sir, wouldn't Bobby be better than me?' Finn suggested this on a note of naïve hope. 'Bobby's such a high-powered egghead type.' Finn paused to consider this designation, and appeared to feel that it might be regarded as offensively derogatory. 'Not that one would really notice it, of course,' he added. 'The world thinks of Bobby as a bloody good man behind a scrum.'

'I hope Bobby is properly appreciative of the compliment. Have you met Giles's father, Rupert Ashmore of King's Yatter?'

'I did meet him once, sir. Smooth type.'

'Precisely. He is the man who stands to gain most, you know, by his elder brother Martyn's sudden death. They were a very long-lived family, the Ashmores. Rupert might have reckoned on continuing to have an elder brother for anything up to thirty years. And Rupert is said to be rather impoverished. He has no doubt been wishing Martyn dead.'

'Oh, I –' Finn checked himself. 'Do you think he picked up that fire-dog –'

'Perhaps he did. But I have an idea that Rupert Ashmore's mind moves more obliquely than that. Not necessarily less effectively.' Appleby swung the wheel and turned into a narrow lane. 'You know that Ashmores have a habit of marrying and propagating very late in life?'

'Yes, sir. What might be called the Robina-complex.'

'Just that. I have a feeling that Rupert Ashmore hasn't much wanted his brother Martyn to marry and propagate.'

'Obviously not. And that would go for Giles as well.'

'Indeed it would. Incidentally, Finn, you yourself speak of Miss Bunker in what I'd call an aggressively hard-boiled way. Didn't you –?'

'That was all rot.' Finn spoke with a sudden violent energy. 'But perhaps you have me typed as seething with jealous rage against all Ashmores?'

'Let's stick to Rupert for a moment. He called on me yesterday, accompanied by the young Frenchman –'

'Jules de Voisin. Equally smooth in his own way.'

'Well, yes. I'm not sure that Jules wasn't tumbling to things of which he didn't approve. I first met him hot on the scent of something of the kind. But the main point is that Rupert would be for slow and devious courses. It seems to be otherwise with the third brother, Ambrose. I've been hearing about him. A picturesquely violent man. And probably quite mad.'

'They're all quite mad, one way or another. Take the scheme that Giles latched on to – the present of wine, and all that. Amusing to suggest to a chap, and egg him on to. But crazy to act out, so to speak.'

'But wasn't it Giles's impression that it had worked?'

'Yes – but that was just the more fool Giles, once again. The old man was laughing at him.'

'And then *this* happened – what we are facing now. But what you, Finn, are facing – just at this moment – is Ambrose. Ambrose Ashmore *chez lui*. And this must be the drive.'

17

'May I have fuller instructions, please?'

Finn said this as he prepared to get out of the car. Appleby, instead of turning up the drive of Abbot's Yatter, had gone on for a hundred yards and parked unobtrusively behind a high hedge.

'Very well. Listen.' Appleby talked rapidly for a couple of minutes. 'Now, hand me that revolver,' he said. He slipped the weapon into a pocket, and watched Finn move off, not very briskly, in the direction of Ambrose Ashmore's lair. 'Don't forget about the field path,' he called after him. Finn, without turning round, gave a perfunctory wave. Appleby watched him go, and then fished out an Ordnance Survey map. The new series, he recalled, had paths where there was an uncontested right-of-way printed in red. This made the present operation less chancy. He wasn't sure that he didn't feel a certain compunction about Finn. It wouldn't be pleasant to look back and realize that he had treated the young man as expendable. But that was an over-dramatic view of the situation. Indeed, there probably *wasn't* a situation – not here at Abbot's Yatter. It was a long time since he had moved so extravagantly on a mere hunch. He fell to studying the map with care.

Finn walked up the drive. Or rather he strolled up the drive, since he remembered that he was on an undirected rural ramble. He paused to stare with a kind of ignorant interest at some cows, moved on, rounded a bend, and had his goal before him. Abbot's Yatter, despite the ancient suggestion of its name, was a modern brick house of the incongruously suburban sort that is sometimes pitched down in the middle of an unoffending country-side. Its perpetrator had perhaps been ashamed of it, for it now stood amid a huddle of hastily grown Austrian pines. These gave it a furtive look, as if it were hoping to escape observation altogether. Perhaps the place was ashamed of not appearing more prosperous than it did. The wood-work stood in need of a coat of paint. The garden, which was large, hinted various adaptations and make-shift arrangements to reduce the need of labour. There was no sign of life.

The front door was defended by an ecclesiastical-looking porch and a variety of repellent objects for scraping boots on. There was a twisty wrought iron bell-pull, and Finn gave a tug at it. Somewhere in the depths of the house this produced an effect as of many tin cans being kicked around a large void space. It also prompted several dogs to yap, bark, or growl. Presently the door opened upon an elderly woman dressed in black. What they call an upper servant, Finn thought. He peered past her into a large gloomy hall. It had shiny tiles, with here and there some unfortunate animal flattened out in order to make a rug. There was an enormous black bear on its hind legs and still in the round; it looked so extremely ferocious that one was surprised to observe it politely holding out a brass salver – no doubt in the expectation of a shower of visiting-cards. There was a bit of an elephant – in fact a leg amputated at the knee, if elephants have knees – for people to put umbrellas or fishing-rods in. Finn had no doubt that more leisured scrutiny would reveal further objects of equal cheer. But this was not allowed.

'Well?' the woman in black said.

'Oh, good morning.' (Finn doubted whether the best upper servants say 'Well?' just like that.) 'Is Mr Giles at home?'

'Giles? There's no Mr Giles here.'

'I asked whether Mr Giles is at home.' Remembering his instructions, Finn bellowed this as if he had every reason to suppose the woman deaf. 'Mr Giles Ashmore. I'm a friend of his.'

'You very well may be. But you've come to the wrong house.'

'The wrong house?' Finn shouted. 'This is King's Yatter, isn't it?'

'Nothing of the sort.'

'But I was *told* it was King's Yatter.'

'This is Abbot's Yatter, the residence of Mr Ambrose Ashmore.'

'Is he at home? Can I see him? I'm sure there must be a mistake. About my friend Giles.' As Finn said this – he had to take deep breaths between sentences in order to keep up what he judged to be an adequate racket – he became aware of a shaft of light at the back of the hideous hall. Somebody had opened a door. Finn took a step backwards into sunlight, and looked first this way and then that. It was essential that he should be clearly identifiable. 'You see, I was told that Giles lives at King's Yatter.'

'So he does. And I tell you this is Abbot's Yatter. Haven't you got ears to your head?'

'Then I've made a mistake?' Finn stared at the woman in a manner so exaggeratedly imbecile that she took a step backward in her turn.

'You want King's Yatter,' the woman said. 'The residence of Mr Ashmore's brother, and no doubt of Mr Giles Ashmore as well. Good morning.'

'But will you please tell me how to get there? I don't know this part of the world at all. Is there a nice field path to King's Yatter? I don't often get into the country. So, when I do, I try –'

'I know nothing about field paths. Go back to the road, and turn right, and watch the sign-posts.'

'I'd much rather ramble through the fields.' Finn fancied he heard a man's voice say something from the back of the hall. 'I wonder whether Mr Ashmore – *your* Mr Ashmore – could help me? May I see him, please?'

'Just wait here,' the woman in black said ungraciously, and shut the front door in Finn's face. She had certainly received some more or less covert summons from her employer. And after a couple of minutes she opened the door again. 'Mr Ashmore is engaged.' she said. 'But I'm to give you a message. Go round to the back of the house, and through the white gate. Cross the field and take the path through the wood. It's about two miles to King's Yatter.'

'Thank you very much.' Finn fancied he heard, somewhere at the side of the house, the engine of a car start into life. He turned away from the front door – it was already closed again – and made his way in the direction of the sound. Whatever the vehicle was, it had vanished. He went on to the back of the house, and through a yard. There, sure enough, was a white gate, and beyond it a faint track going diagonally across a field. Finn followed the directions he had been given.

The October day was now filled with bright sunshine. It had the odd effect of turning the grass – which everyone knows to be permanently green – to primrose colour. Finn found this quite pleasant; it was like looking at a decent Impressionist painting. But there was a striking contrast when he reached the wood. He wasn't fifty yards into it when he saw that it was a nasty sort of place. He couldn't name the trees, but they were very close together, and went up a very long way, and at the top were so abundant in leaves or something that very little light came through. It was very quiet. Finn couldn't hear his own footsteps, because of some soft sort of carpeting he was walking on. But every now and then a twig snapped in the middle distance – just as in a novel when the author wants to turn on a spot of suspense.

A spot of suspense, as a matter of fact, *had* been turned on. Finn felt it as something doing things with his spine. He wasn't in the least unaware of what this rural ramble was in aid of, and he felt that he ought to be cursing Bobby Appleby's father roundly; either that, or simply turning round and walking out of this whole Ashmore business altogether. Not that that might be entirely wise. It was conceivably what Giles had done – and perhaps it was the way to get yourself tapped on the shoulder by a policeman. He had better go on. It was rather fun, as a matter of fact. Perhaps his heart was feeling it to be rather fun. Perhaps that was why it was bumping inside his chest.

He wished he hadn't formed that suspicion about Bobby's father being a bit past it. One wants, in a spot like this, to be pretty sure –

Finn found that he had come to a halt. It wasn't because he had heard anything, or because anything had moved. For nearly half a mile the trees had been pressing close around him, for his path barely had an independent existence in their midst. But now, only a dozen yards ahead, he was going to pass through a glade. He believed that was the word for it: an oval clearing perhaps just large enough to contain a tennis-court. Finn wondered why he had thought of tennis-court, which was something nobody would think to plank down in a god-forsaken spot like this. The path made a distinguishable track across the glade – following its narrower axis: where the net would be, you might say. There was no need, of course, to follow it exactly. Indeed, there was no need to enter the glade at all. It would be perfectly sensible to skirt it, keeping among the trees. More shady, for instance. Cooler. Finn took a deep breath, and walked straight ahead.

This proved to be a good thing, because it was all over in an instant. First there was an angry shout, and then a very loud report, and in the same instant as that a curiously ugly tearing sound high up in the trees ahead of him. Then he heard the voice of Bobby's father saying – very calmly – 'Put it down, I'm armed.' There was a moment's silence, in which Finn could just hear the sound of heavy breathing. Then Appleby spoke again. 'This way, Finn. There's an acquaintance of yours here.'

158

Finn looked from Appleby's prisoner – and as he did so his hand went instinctively to his jaw. It was true that there was no bruise. But it still ached. And here was the chap who had punched it. This time, he hadn't judged a fist adequate to the job on hand. On the ground near where he stood there lay a sporting rifle. Appleby had a foot on it.

'Your ferocious friend, I think?' Appleby said.

'Absolutely. Not a doubt about it.'

'And not a doubt that he is Mr Ambrose Ashmore – who reads detective stories, and knows that one must obliterate fingerprints. He may even know that it is worth taking a very stiff risk indeed to liquidate a fatally damaging witness.'

'Me?' Finn said. Although he had so clearly known himself not to be in the dark about what he had just been put through, he noticed that it was now his stomach rather than his spine that something was happening to.

'Demonstrably, my dear Finn.'

'I have the hang of it, sir. At least, I think I have. But how did you know?'

'I can't be said to have known. It would be quite wildly the wrong word. But I had a notion. *For a moment, I had a queer impression it was Giles.*'

'*What?*'

'You remember saying that? Mr Ambrose Ashmore here is about three times his nephew's age. Still, family likenesses sometimes do flash out. So I told myself that the fellow who knocked you out might well have been an Ashmore. I don't know much about the tribe – although my wife has a good deal to tell about them. But I do happen to know that our friend here' – and Appleby nodded towards the silent and glowering Ambrose – 'may be described as the ferocious one. That, again, was your word for the chap who took a smack at you.'

'Just how ferocious?' Finn asked.

'A very good question, Finn. Answering it accurately

may take us quite a long way. At least he has a violent temper: horse-whips his garden-boy and pitches his wife's *chef* through a window. That sort of thing. It struck me that, if it was he last night, he might already be regretting that he hadn't been a little more definitively – I think we may put it that way – violent when you found him emerging from the Chase –'

'Emerging? Definitely that?'

'No, Finn; it's only a hypothesis. I'm just telling you – and our friend here – how my mind worked. Or what's left of my mind . . . My dear lad, have I embarrassed you?'

'Of course not,' Finn said. And he added desperately: 'I don't know what you mean.'

'Let us stick to hypotheses. Mr Ashmore – this Mr Ashmore – is suddenly confronted last night by a total stranger. This happens when he is in an awkward situation. We needn't pause over the degree of awkwardness. Various terms will have to be considered' – Appleby glanced again at Ambrose Ashmore – 'such as "compromising" and "incriminating". But we may leave that aside. The point is that, in this admittedly difficult moment of time, he miscalculates. He decides that a sock on the jaw will do. He neglects the fact that the stranger he knocks out in this way may bob up again – next day, next week, next year – and confront him. How will he react, if and when this confrontation takes place? I think it may be said that we've been devoting part of the morning to find out.' Appleby smiled. 'But please don't feel, Finn, that you've been in all that physical danger. Of course my mental processes are becoming very slow. But simple physical action – say, throwing up a man's rifle in a split instant of time – is still quite reasonably within my command. It comes of a tolerably sober life. And now I think we'll return to the Chase. All three of us.'

'Yes, of course.' Finn was staring at Ambrose Ashmore as if fascinated by a snake. 'Sir,' he said, 'does all this mean that this man had just killed his brother? It's something there's a word for, isn't there?'

'Fratricide, Finn. But I don't think I want to answer your question.' Appleby paused, and looked at the young man sombrely. 'We mustn't run too far ahead, you know.'

18

'Isn't that Ambrose Ashmore in your car?' Colonel Pride asked. 'And with the young fellow called Finn?'

'That's right.' Once more, Appleby looked round the room in which Martyn Ashmore had died. 'It's the ferocious Ambrose. And Finn is guarding him.'

'Ferocious? Well, he's known to have the devil of a temper. But why should Finn be guarding him? Why should he put up with such a thing?'

'Finn is guarding him because he's on our murder-list. And he's putting up with it because he's scared. Not that he is without what may be called a truculent story. He took a gun out this morning over some land where he has shooting rights. And I jumped on him with a revolver, accused him of trying to kill Finn, and have brought him to the Chase by a wholly illegal use of force.'

'Well, I'll be damned!' Colonel Pride produced a handkerchief and mopped his brow. '*Did* he try to kill Finn?'

'It might be possible to maintain that he only proposed to intimidate him. I don't say it would be true. But it could be maintained.'

'My dear John, whatever are you getting at?'

'Ambrose was here last night. It was he who gave the prowling Finn that clip on the jaw. There are, no doubt, various stories that Ambrose can tell. It may be possible to strike a bargain with him. We take a lenient – even phoney – view of his exploit this morning in exchange for as much of the truth as is in him about last night. If he *didn't* kill his brother, it may be a useful line.'

'I've never heard of anything more outrageously irregular!'

'That, Tommy, is why you and I are alone in this room. Shall we invite Mr Ambrose Ashmore to join us for a quiet chat?'

'I don't know that anything of the sort ought to take place except in the presence of at least one of my officers. Things might turn very awkward, if we –'

'We'll have Finn, instead of one of your henchmen. A confrontation, you know. I'd say it was essential. And it would help if you strolled out and brought them in. I'm afraid Ambrose doesn't care for me very much.'

The truth of this became apparent a couple of minutes later. Preceded by Colonel Pride, and followed by Finn, Ambrose Ashmore entered the room, violently expostulating.

'Pride,' he said, 'I call upon you to arrest this scoundrel. Assault and abduction.'

'Of course I take note of what you say, Mr Ashmore. Won't you sit down? Mr Finn, sit down too – and don't speak until you are spoken to.'

'Thank you, sir.' Finn sat down demurely.

'Fellow calls himself Sir John Something,' Ambrose said. 'Never heard of him. Never set eyes on him.'

'And Mr Finn?' Pride asked, and indicated the young man. 'Have you ever set eyes on him?'

'I decline to be interrogated.' If Ambrose was indeed scared, it was plain that he was quite genuinely angry as well. Perhaps it would have been better to say 'enraged'. There were veins standing out in an ugly way at his temples. But possibly, Appleby thought, this was his habitual emotional state. Solo Hoobin had been very rash ever to enter his employment.

'It is Mr Finn's contention,' Pride went on, 'that you and he had an encounter, here at the Chase, late last night ... You know, by the way, that your brother Martyn is dead?'

The ruthlessness of this took Appleby's breath away. But was it, or was it not, a genuine surprise and shock that Ambrose Ashmore registered in the ensuing moments? Appleby judged it not easy to decide.

'Mr Martyn Ashmore,' Pride was continuing presently, 'died last night in this room, and in circumstances which must occasion suspicion of foul play. So the matter of your alleged encounter with Mr Finn is of the gravest import. It will be wise, Mr Ashmore, that for the moment we should neglect whatever has been happening this morning, and concentrate on last night. Mr Finn declares that he came upon you at the front door of this house, and that you knocked him unconscious. Mr Finn may be offering me a complete fabrication. Or he may be genuinely mistaken as to your identity. If you deny having been here – which may be the truth – there must inevitably be much further investigation. If you agree that you were here, that clears so much of the ground, and we can turn to other aspects of the situation confronting us.'

'It is possible,' Appleby said, 'that you are aware of something in your own situation that is embarrassing or even legally dubious and morally reprehensible. Or perhaps merely of something that testifies to a humiliating failure of nerve. But I think I ought to point out that prevarication at this point, if it were to be proved against you –'

'What do you mean – proved against me?' This was the first time that Ambrose Ashmore had directly addressed Appleby.

'There were other people around the Chase last night. And at least two of them – I need mention only your brother's gamekeeper – would have recognized you the moment they saw you. And if you were proved, I repeat, to be telling lies, your position might be compromised in the most dreadful way.'

'He means,' Finn interrupted scandalously, 'that you'd be where, in the old days, you'd swing for it.'

'Mr Finn, I told you to be quiet.' Colonel Pride glared at the young man, but there was something in his eye that signalled covert approval of this brutal turn of the screw. And it was now Ambrose who was mopping his brow.

'Out with it,' Finn said encouragingly.

'I was here. And I did hit out at this young man. I don't know who the devil he is. As for this morning, I had no notion of doing him any harm.' Ambrose hesitated. 'Just of suggesting to him that it would be healthy if he cleared out.'

'Mr Ashmore,' Colonel Pride said mildly, 'you appear to be, on your own confession, a person of the most ungoverned impulses towards violence and intimidation.'

'In a man of your age,' Finn said, feeling his jaw, 'it's a damned unbecoming thing.'

Appleby was glancing out of the window. He saw that Bobby had arrived. But he wasn't alone; instead of the missing Giles Ashmore, he had provided himself with a young woman. She was good-looking, and she was quite clearly another Ashmore. Bobby seemed to be expostulating with a police sergeant about not being admitted to his father's presence forthwith. Appleby sighed, and glanced at his watch.

'I think,' he said briskly, 'that Mr Ashmore wants to make a preliminary statement about his presence at the Chase last night. But perhaps "statement" is too formal a word. At this stage, we needn't write anything down. Mr Ashmore, I understand that you and your brothers were not on the best of terms, and saw each other comparatively rarely. So why did you come to the Chase late last night?'

'Because of that damned girl!' Ambrose Ashmore, casting caution aside, produced this in a kind of infuriated shout. 'Some jumped-up caterwauling kitchen-maid – not that that's either here or there – who was going to marry my brother Rupert's fool of a son. Then yesterday morning, in *The Times* –'

'Quite so. You came to the Chase to expostulate with your brother Martyn over the announcement of his engagement to Miss Bunker. But it can't be said, can it, that you had a very strong case?'

'What the devil do you mean?'

'In the light of family tradition, let us say. Ashmores often marry rather late in life – and start begetting children in their seventies or eighties. That was the trouble, I take it?'

'Of course it was the trouble!' Ambrose said this with a frankness that was almost disarming. 'Martyn was letting me down badly.'

'And letting your brother Rupert and his son Giles down badly too?'

'Yes, of course. But these people can look after themselves.'

'I met your brother Rupert yesterday – and a young Frenchman who is going to marry his daughter. Can you tell me where Rupert is now?'

'Of course I can't. His movements are nothing to me.'

'I see. Then may we come back to your own movements last night? You saw your brother Martyn?'

'Yes, I did.' Ambrose looked uneasily about the room. 'He let me into the house, and we came in here.'

'And what did he say about his proposed marriage?'

'He said it was no business of mine. He laughed at me.'

'You quarrelled?'

'Yes.'

'A violent quarrel, Mr Ashmore – quite in your usual style?'

'I don't know what you mean. I came away. I let myself out of the house, and found myself confronted by this young man. I admit that, and that I did knock him down. I was very much upset, you see.'

'It was quite a natural thing for one of your violent temperament to do. But was it only because you had been in dispute with your brother that you thought to wipe the door-handle and door-bell clear of fingerprints?'

'I did nothing of the kind.' Ambrose Ashmore's voice rose a pitch.

'Mr Finn says you were doing that.'

'Then your Mr Finn is talking nonsense.'

'Very well.' Appleby made a long pause. 'Mr Ashmore, was your brother alive when you left him?'

'Of course he was alive.' Ambrose moistened his lips. 'I want to see my solicitor.'

'Then you had better go and do so. I am sure the Chief Constable will put a car at your disposal. And I have only one other question to ask you. After your dispute with your brother, and after your rash assault – your *first* rash assault – upon Mr Finn, did you, or did you not, remain near, or return to, the Chase last night?'

'I neither remained nor returned. I went straight home.'

'Mr Ashmore, thank you very much.'

'I don't think he's telling the truth,' Appleby said. 'Or he was scared enough to tell some of it, and too scared to tell it all. But if what he has suppressed is what I think it is, there's something devilishly wrong with our whole approach to the affair. Oh cursed spite, that ever I was born to set it right.'

'My dear fellow,' Pride said soothingly, 'your assistance is invaluable.'

Appleby chuckled, turned away from the window, and frowned into the empty fireplace.

'Surely,' he said, 'Rupert Ashmore should have been located by now? We want him on the spot – together with his runaway son and that young Frenchman. Talking of sons, I'm going out to have a word with Bobby. Finn, you'd better lose yourself.'

'Oh, I say!'

'But not for too long. I may want you again. Even the Chief Constable may want you again.' He turned to Pride. 'That girl out there,' he said. 'I've guessed who she is. Rupert's daughter Virginia. I'll see if there's anything I can get out of her.'

19

'This is my father,' Bobby Appleby said to the girl. 'I think you ought to talk to him. I'll be strolling round the place.'

'Don't go too far, Bobby.' Appleby glanced curiously at his son. 'And talk to Finn. He's feeling disapproved of. Miss Ashmore, shall we take a turn in the park?' Appleby led the way down a flight of steps. 'Of course you know of your uncle's death?'

'Your son told me. And I said I would like to be brought over to the Chase. Has my father turned up here?'

'Not yet. The police are trying to contact him. Can you help them, by any chance?'

'I don't think so. It seems very probable that my father has run away. Does that sound insane?'

'I should like to think it did.',

'I have only just discovered that I live among mad people. Or I have only just admitted it to myself.' Miss Ashmore, although clearly in some state of extreme tension, said this quite calmly. 'It makes one do stupid things. For example, I have told your son some perfectly useless lies.'

'Useless lies are not commonly very bad ones.'

'One was that Jules – who is known as my fiancé – would look after the dogs while I came over here. It wasn't true. Jules has departed.'

'You mean that he has run away like your father?'

'Not quite that. He quarrelled with my father yesterday afternoon –'

'Miss Ashmore, you really are a quarrelsome crowd.'

'I agree. And it was *quite* mad. It wasn't because – as I've discovered – my father had been doing something unspeakably cruel and wildly criminal.' Miss Ashmore's voice had become icy. 'It was because the rationality of the French nation was being aspersed. Jules came and told me the facts, read me a lecture on them, packed his bags, and departed.'

'I think, perhaps, you had better tell *me* the facts.'

'Very well. This is something else I lied to your son about. My Uncle Martyn, it seems, had dreadful experiences during the war – and also, in France, for some years afterwards. It had left him with a neurosis, an *idée fixe* – I'm not sure what it should be called. And my father has been working upon it, causing strange and sinister things to happen, in order to drive Uncle Martyn slowly mad – or to have him tell such an unlikely story that he would be *thought* to be mad –'

'Yes.' Appleby thought he might well interrupt at this point. 'Your father has struck me as a man whose methods would be oblique or devious.'

'Then, only a few days ago, one of these silly and wicked pranks went wrong. My father was stupid enough to do something before a witness –'

'Quite so. It was an enormous mistake, and perhaps the product of a sudden access of real homicidal feeling. Incidentally, I was the witness. And Jules, Miss Ashmore?'

'He simply decided he couldn't take it, and asked for his cards. I don't blame him. Only, I suspect he was aware of what had been happening, in a general way. He only started creating because he had a thing about France.'

'It's to the credit of a Frenchman that he should have a thing about France. Do I understand you to regard your engagement as broken off?'

'Most decidedly.'

'I think you now know about another broken engagement? At least, I suppose it must be called that. I mean your brother Giles's relationship with Miss Bunker, and how your Uncle Martyn appears to have disrupted it?

Presumably your father knows about it too by now. Have you any idea when he found out?'

'He was very upset yesterday afternoon, after he had been looking through the newspapers.'

'I see. And that was before his quarrel with Jules?'

'In a way, yes. But something had been blowing up for some days.'

'May I return to the subject of your father? Why should you judge it probable that he has run away?'

'If he knows about Uncle Martyn's death – about it's being sinister, I mean. If investigation turned up the fact that he himself had been faking attempts on his brother's life, and so on, he would be in a very awkward situation.'

'He certainly would. Although it is entirely uncertain that he does know about his brother's death, so far. When did you last see your father?'

'Isn't that the title of a famous painting?' Miss Ashmore had smiled faintly. 'It was late yesterday afternoon. He said something about his dentist. Then he just got into his car, and drove off. He's often very casual about such things.'

'And he hasn't come home? Surely he wouldn't spend the night at his dentist's?'

'That would be most unusual, I suppose.' There was a note of what might have been sudden desperate fatigue in Miss Ashmore's voice. 'It's a London dentist. My father would spend the night in town. So his running away is not proven, so far. I imagine the same thing holds true of Giles.'

'We at least know just when Giles took himself out of the picture. As you must have heard, my son Bobby saw him off on the midnight train. Perhaps your father and brother will come back together.'

'Perhaps.'

'Miss Ashmore, you have done right to tell me what you have. But the situation must be extremely painful to you. Had you better go home – where your mother is possibly in anxiety by this time? Bobby will take you back. Or I can find a police car.'

'Thank you very much. But, please, not yet. For a little time, Sir John, I think I want to be alone. I'll walk round the park. That will bring me back to the house in about half an hour.' Virginia Ashmore smiled wanly. 'Perhaps the mystery will have solved itself by then.'

'It won't have solved *itself*, Miss Ashmore.' Appleby looked at the girl steadily, and spoke gravely. 'But it may be solved – even in so short a time as thirty minutes.'

'You mean you know –?' The girl's very lovely eyes had rounded perceptibly as she spoke.

'What I chiefly know is that the temporal dimensions of this affair are confusing. Some things, like your father's campaign against your uncle's nervous balance, seem to have been building up for years. Then much happens in a few days – and, after that, even more in a few hours. But just how many hours? It's the next thing I want to find out.'

'The girl has gone off by herself,' Appleby said to Bobby. 'I think we'll keep clear of her for a time. She has the devil of a lot on her plate, poor child.'

'Perhaps her Frenchman will sustain her.' Bobby said this with unconvincing casualness. 'De Voisin, you know.'

'I do know. But there is something she didn't tell you. Pride, I suppose. De Voisin has walked out on her.'

'The low hound!'

'Well, yes. But the fact is he couldn't take the knowledge – or a substantially enlarged knowledge – of some freakish and blackguardly tricks his future father-in-law had been up to. All these people are a really awful crowd.'

'The girl isn't.'

'I think she might stick by them at a pinch, Bobby. But at least this Jules de Voisin is out. As long as he was going to marry Virginia Ashmore, he had an interest in the distribution of the Ashmore property. It would be a feasible motive for murder of the totally calculating and cold-blooded sort. But the moment he broke with these people, the motive vanished.'

'He did come over here last night. It's the final thing we know about him. He said he brought his kinsman a small farewell present.'

'We must presume his present was just the nasty truth about his kinsman's precious brother Rupert. No vengeance and nemesis from those *Résistance* days long ago. Just brother Rupert being utterly diabolical.'

'Would that upset Martyn, do you think, or be a kind of relief to him?'

'Upset him, I think. Do you know? That morning, when I was up on the roof with him and with de Voisin, there was a moment in which I thought his belief in his own interpretation of these episodes – call it the Croix de Lorraine interpretation – faltered. And his confidence faltered with it. Looking back, I can almost see him as clinging to a fantasy – but feeling, in the depth of his mind, that it was his own kindred who were after him.'

'How utterly ghastly! But if some revelation of de Voisin's upset him last night, he was composed enough when Giles took me in to be introduced to him. I had a sense of his feeling he was in command of something.'

'Well, the main point is that de Voisin had ceased to have the slightest occasion to return later and kill him. It's one elimination, and that's something.'

'What about this chap you and the Chief Constable were interviewing when I drove up with Virginia – the younger surviving brother, isn't he, Ambrose?'

'The violent Ambrose. I don't think Ambrose was in on Rupert's plot. Rupert's plot belongs to the region – come to think of it – of slow poisonings. Not Ambrose Ashmore's style. And I think Ambrose has told a good deal of truth about himself. He came storming over to the Chase last night, hard upon reading of Martyn's engagement. He says he *found* his brother alive, had a flaming row, *left* his brother alive – and relieved his baffled feelings, so to speak, against your friend Finn's jaw. There is a certain logical reason why his story *ought* to be true. But I find myself not believing it – not believing the whole of it – all the same.'

'You believe he may really have killed his brother in a passion?'

'That doesn't follow. But I want to avoid that girl in the park. Let's simply walk round the house.' Appleby came to a halt. 'By Jove, no! First of all, we'll go in again – unobtrusively.'

'You mean, avoiding the eye of Tommy Pride's men?'

'Why not? They might want to be helpful, and only succeed in being puzzled. I've had an idea.'

'Oh, I say!' Bobby produced Finn's exclamation with cheerful irreverence. 'It's a bit of a thrill, you know. I've never had a close-up view of Sir John in action before.'

'Don't be a young idiot. What about this door? It's open, all right. Crazy place, the Chase. What we want is the cellarage. This way.'

'Whatever do you want that for?'

'To make ghostly noises from, and startle Colonel Thomas Pride upstairs. Mind these steps; they're tricky. I've been down here before.' Appleby located and flicked on a light-switch.

'Good Lord!' Bobby said.

'Exactly. This is the Newcastle to which your hopeful companion Giles Ashmore brought his coal in the form of a dozen of claret. The stuff isn't upstairs, so my guess is that Uncle Martyn brought it straight down here and dumped it in a bin. I'd just like to check on it.'

'Here's claret,' Bobby said, and started puffing dust from a bottle. 'Holy smoke! Château Margaux '47.'

'I had Lafite '49.' Appleby chuckled. 'And here's what we're looking for. The whole dozen, just standing on end.'

'I can't see that tells you anything.' Bobby turned round. 'Is the champagne there too?'

'Champagne?'

'It seems Giles went the whole hog, and had half a

dozen bottles of champagne shoved in the bottom of the box. It made it uncommonly heavy.'

'There isn't much champagne down here.' Appleby poked around for a couple of minutes. 'Louis Roederer *Cristal Brut*. I think it improbable that our young friend bought that in Linger – or anywhere else. We'll go upstairs again. In fact, back into the open air. I need a breath of it.'

20

Finn was mooning around an untidy yard at the back of the house. He halted as the two Applebys came up to him.

'Ancient sort of place,' he said. 'Did you know there was an old well?'

'A well?' Bobby said. 'When I took a jump from the terrace last night I had a sudden notion I had fallen into the darkness of a well. But of course I hadn't. Where's the real one?'

'Over here.' Finn led the way to a corner of the yard. 'I've just taken off its wooden lid. There's nothing to fasten it down. Dangerous, in a way. Tumble down that, and you wouldn't come up again.'

They peered down the well. They dropped a stone, and there was a faint *plop*.

'Some water still,' Bobby said. 'Good place to get rid of something. Say, half a dozen of champagne.'

'What's that?' Finn was startled.

'Your friend Giles's claret's in the house, but his champagne has vanished. Martyn Ashmore must have so disliked the sight of it that he brought it out and pitched it down this well. The last act of his life.'

'What macabre rubbish!' Finn was indignant. 'Convenient for dumping *something*, all the same. Shall we insist that Colonel Pride sends down one of his coppers? I don't mind giving a hand to lower the rope.'

'Embers,' Appleby said suddenly. 'Ashes.'

The two young men stared at him.

'The fire is the key, you know. A brisk log fire in Ashmore's room. Bobby, you saw it from the hall? And you both saw it through the window?'

'Yes, of course.'

'We've been timing Ashmore's death on the assumption that the fire had gone out before it happened – simply because he was lying in the ashes, without so much as his hair being singed. A couple of hours at least after you had a last glimpse of him. Only, as I said before, there's been something devilishly wrong with our way of looking at the thing. Oh cursed spite, in fact. Finn, you follow me?'

'I can't say I do, sir.' Finn looked excessively blank.

'It was Hamlet's feeling that the time was out of joint. *Our* time has been out of joint. That's all.' Appleby paused. 'For suppose somebody simply raked out the fire – shoved the whole flaming mass into a big bucket, and really did chuck it down this well? He'd only have to rake dead ash and a charred stump or two from the back of that big fireplace –'

'The chap who took the swipe at me!' Finn said. 'And then the pot shot this morning. The swipe was one thing. But the pot-shot was quite another. He wouldn't feel I needed murdering if he'd merely encountered me after he'd had a row with his brother.'

'There is much force in that,' Appleby said. 'I can't believe that Ambrose Ashmore hasn't been feeling in an uncommonly hazardous situation. Still, it isn't necessary to suppose he killed his brother. He may merely have found him dead. Not only dead, but apparently bludgeoned. Wiping away fingerprints, socking an intrusive young man, taking a gun to the same young man – doubly intrusive – next day: these things would flow reasonably enough from the sense of being in so tight a spot. There was his reputation as a thoroughly violent character, for one thing.'

'But,' Bobby said slowly, 'if Ambrose did no more than walk into the Chase in a temper and find his brother dead, who does that leave us with?'

'The remaining inhabitants of the British Isles, more or less.' Appleby had turned away from the well, and was making once more for the front of the house. 'Plus Monsieur Jules de Voisin. And plus, if you like, vengeful members of the *Maquis*. That option's still open.'

'For practical purposes, surely, we're left with anybody who had a motive for killing the old man – and who hasn't an alibi.' Bobby paused until they had rounded an angle of the house. 'What about the brother who is due to inherit this place – Rupert?'

'Perhaps his dentist will provide *him* with an alibi,' Appleby said. 'I've known it happen.'

'His son Giles?'

'Oh, I say!' Finn had halted in his tracks. 'We've been *running* Giles, sir. Bobby and I, that is. Giles couldn't take an effective bash at anybody.'

'He could have got back into the house, Finn.' Appleby too had halted, and he was looking at Finn with gravity. 'When you all three scattered because of Ibell –'

'Ibell, sir? But he was an unrehearsed effect. Giles couldn't have reckoned on him.'

'I rather question that. Ibell had his regular round.'

'At least I don't believe that Giles could have had time to manage that mucky fire-dousing business. I think Giles is out. But what about the girl?'

'The girl,' Bobby repeated quickly. 'What girl?'

'The girl wandering round the park now.' Finn pointed into distance. 'The girl – Giles's sister – who seems to have insisted on revisiting the scene of the crime. Bobby, you brought her over, didn't you?'

'Certainly I did. And what the hell are you talking about?' Bobby Appleby was looking at his friend Finn as if he had suddenly become his blackest enemy. 'What sort of motive does *she* have?'

'All Ashmores, male or female, had some sort of motive for eliminating nasty old Martyn.' Finn spoke without confidence. 'But keep your shirt on. Only an idle thought. Count me out, old man, on the detective stakes.'

'What about yourself, for that matter?' Bobby had squared up to Finn positively dangerously. 'Left slinking around the Chase, weren't you, last night? And wildly wounded in your bleeding vanity because old Martyn Ashmore had stolen the girl who'd already been stolen from you by that silly sod Giles?'

'My dear lads,' Appleby murmured, 'please do remember that something quite serious is going on. Bobby, will you pipe down? And, Finn, the same to you.'

'Sorry,' Finn said. 'I'll go and cool off.' He made towards Bobby an entirely amiable gesture which consisted in clenching a fist and brandishing it in air. 'Be seeing you, sir.' And he marched off.

'Really, Bobby!' Appleby glanced ruefully at his son. 'I respect you immensely as a young man bowled over by a beautiful girl. Good luck to you.'

'You said they're an awful crowd – the Ashmores. You wouldn't want to see me mixed up with them?'

'The Ravens were, at the least, extremely eccentric. I plunged straight in.' Appleby paused – then, seeing Bobby flush, he hurried on. 'Let's stick to the point. I really want your help in another character. Come round to the front of the house.' He glanced at his watch. 'I said something rash to Miss Ashmore about half an hour. There isn't a great deal of it left.'

'In your character as a novelist,' Appleby said seriously. They were standing on the terrace, and in front of them was the window of the room in which Martyn Ashmore had died. 'The same sort of novelist, more or less, as Alain Robbe-Grillet.'

'Go on,' Bobby said. He had a quick instinct for moments at which he wasn't being made fun of.

'Do you know, I was reading aloud to your mother from that chap the other evening? And I can remember at least a fragment of it. *Since its width is the same for the central portion as for the sides, the line of shadow cast by the column extends precisely to the corner of the house.*'

'Do you mean' – Bobby was staring at the window – 'that there is some specific significance in that quotation?'

'Not in the least. What interests me is the discipline, the bent of mind. Get the tangible and visible universe right, and everything else will shine through. That seems to me the notion. It demands the cultivation of a habit, I take it, of seeing what is really there – the *whole* of what is really there?'

'Naturally.'

'Then – *look*.' Appleby was pointing at the window. 'Of course, the curtains were nearly drawn, and that makes a difference. But here you are, out in the darkness with these two worthies beside you, and you are looking in. What do you see?'

There was a long silence. Bobby was not, in fact, looking – or not with his organs of bodily sight. His eyes were shut.

'Clearly an exercise,' he said, 'in visual recall. Like Kim's Game. You remember at children's parties? A tray covered with small objects. You're allowed to look at it for thirty seconds –' He broke off. 'I'm sorry,' he said, 'but I can't see anything out of the way. Only I *ought* to. I can remember that.'

'It must be something very unimpressive, Bobby. Something that not many people would notice at all.'

'And so it is!' Bobby had swung round, and his eyes were now very wide open indeed. 'A most tenuous appearance, one might say.'

'A mere thread of a clue?'

'Almost that.'

'Ariadne's thread, Bobby. It leads to the heart of the labyrinth – and probably to the bottom of that well.'

'Isn't it rather a long shot?'

'Worth one of Tommy's men getting himself a bit mucky. Let's –' Appleby swung round, following Bobby's gaze. 'Ah!' he said. 'Another of the bad pennies has turned up.'

The bad penny was Rupert Ashmore. He had emerged from the house – where it was to be presumed he had already seen the Chief Constable – and was hurrying in Appleby's direction now.

'My dear Sir John, this a very terrible thing!' Rupert had the air of condoling with Appleby on some intimate loss. 'I am deeply grieved – deeply grieved, indeed. It is a great shock. I have only just got back from town, having had to hurry to my dentist in some pain late yesterday. He has put the matter right, you will be glad to know. But why should I speak of such a trifle? That my poor brother should be so suddenly taken! A seizure, it seems. I have been told that they are often instantly fatal to persons of disordered mind. But we must never speak of poor Martyn's affliction again. It is too painful. He was a remarkable man. When I take over the Chase, I shall have a small memorial erected in the park.'

'Before you do that, Mr Ashmore, I have some hope that you will be clapped into gaol.'

'My dear sir!' Rupert's features expressed the largest astonishment. 'Have you taken leave of your senses?'

'Either I, or your unfortunate brother, very nearly took leave of his brains the other morning, as a consequence of your antics up on that roof. I have every hope that intensive investigation will connect you with several similar exploits. And now your brother has actually met a violent end. Your position is unenviable, Mr Ashmore.'

'Where is my daughter Virginia? I demand to see her. She has been carried off – and doubtless constrained to make damaging statements of a wholly baseless sort. By threats and bullying. I insist that she be released.'

'Your daughter is entirely her own mistress, sir. And she is walking somewhere in the park.'

'Where's Finn?' Bobby asked suddenly. 'Finn seems to have wandered off too.'

21

'Good Lord!' Finn said, fifteen minutes later. He had strolled into the stable-yard of Ashmore Chase and come upon the group of men round the well. 'Surely nobody is taking that ploy seriously?' He watched the head and shoulders of a constable disappear into darkness. 'Is that sort of champagne really worth it?'

'You may find it's a pretty odd sort of champagne.' Bobby Appleby had swung round. 'Where on earth have you been? And where is Virginia?'

'I borrowed your car. The key was in the ignition. I hope you don't mind?'

'I've put up with worse than that from you, I suppose.' Bobby sounded resigned. 'But what did you want the car for, anyway?'

'I ran Virginia to that A.A. telephone on the main road. She wanted to make a call.'

'You had been talking to Miss Ashmore?' It was Appleby who had turned round now. With a brisk inclination of the head, he drew the two young men aside. 'You followed her into the park as soon as you left us?'

'Well, yes. I'd got a glimpse of her, you know, and she seemed rather attractive.' Finn offered this explanation with an appearance of entire artlessness. 'And, of course, I thought it might be a time for a chap to rally round. Her family not showing up in too good a light, and so forth.'

'And did she respond to being rallied round?'

'Not too well at first, sir. But I chatted her up.'

'Did you, indeed? May I ask what you judged to be a suitable topic of conversation?'

'Well, just all this.' Finn made a gesture. 'It would have

been silly – it would have been quite artificial, wouldn't it? – to talk about anything else. So I had a go – from a sympathetic viewpoint. Told her the latest, and so on.'

'Just what do you mean by the latest?'

'Well, sir, things like your saying that the fire was the key.'

'Was it at that point that Miss Ashmore said she wanted to make a telephone call?'

'I don't quite remember.' Finn produced his artless look again. Then he caught sight of Appleby's expression, and it vanished.

'Finn, I think you knew very well what you were doing?'

Finn hesitated only for a second.

'Yes, sir. I think she knew where she could contact her brother on the telephone – or leave a message for him.'

'It's your belief that the truth – or an outline of it – had just flashed on her? That she can have known nothing whatever about it until that very moment?'

'That's how it felt. Anything really grim and dark about her brother, I mean. In fact, I'm certain of it. She had tumbled to something that *I* hadn't tumbled to, and it was a terrific shock. She did say something queer – something about Giles having been interested in fires. Anyway, I knew what she was doing.'

'And you knew what *you* were doing? You thought it was right?'

'She had made an appeal to me.' Finn looked straight at Appleby. 'Not explicitly – is that the word? She might just have been wanting to telephone her mama about being home to lunch. But I knew. I knew that she wanted to give her brother a chance. Shall I be put in quod, do you think? There just wasn't anything else I could do.'

'Your incarceration is improbable – or the girl's, for that matter.' Appleby looked at Finn soberly. 'You accepted a heavy responsibility, all the same.'

'Yes, I see that. If it's as I think it is, I believe I know what Giles will do.'

'It's our duty –'

Appleby was interrupted by a shout behind him. They all turned round. The constable, gloriously muddy, had been hauled out of the well. He was clutching a bulky object in his arms.

'The champagne,' Bobby said quietly, 'transformed into something rich and strange.'

'The champagne?' Finn echoed in bewilderment. 'That isn't –'

'My dear Finn, there never was any champagne. Look!' Appleby had pointed. The constable's burden had been set down in the yard, and a certain amount of mud and weed cleared away from it. It stood revealed as a large electric fire: the kind that masquerades as a heap of flaming logs.

*

'When Bobby first peered through the window,' Appleby said to Judith that night, 'he saw the electric flex – which is something an honest-to-God fire doesn't have. But it was simply the visual image that registered, followed by no rational inference at all – and apparently no impress upon his memory. However, he recovered it as soon as I shoved him at the window again – and when something like the truth was beginning to dawn on my own mind.'

'The rather dim-seeming Giles Ashmore is not without resource.'

'Decidedly not. He smuggled the fire into the Chase beneath a dozen bottles of claret. But that was simply to elude the observation of his two companions. Once in Martyn Ashmore's presence, he simply produced it boldly. Ashmore must have been put in good humour by the absurdity of the miserable claret, and he was no doubt in high feather over having out-smarted his nephew with Miss Bunker. So he accepted the contraption graciously, and allowed Giles to fix it up at once. A "very original present", he called it in Bobby's hearing later. There was nothing else of the kind in the house, apart from a wretched little electric radiator in the hall. Incidentally, I don't suppose he often lit a fire at this time of year. But the fireplace had the abundant remains of one, left neglected since goodness knows when. The rest of the story pretty well tells itself.'

'I'm not sure that it tells itself to me.'

'Giles got Bobby into the hall, simply to glimpse that great big fire through a door. He had the good luck to manage that further glimpse through the window. But Ibell, I think, he was reckoning on; and when Bobby and Finn scattered in alarm he simply slipped back into the house, killed his uncle, arranged his head and shoulders in the cold ashes, and took the electric contraption out and pitched it down the well. All he had to do then was to keep up an alibi over a period of so many hours – you may say while that non-existent wood fire was dying down and going out. Hence the whole business of having Bobby see him off to London – non-stop.'

'Do you think that Giles knew about his uncle and Robina?'

'I should judge it extremely probable, and it would add a good deal of extra drive to his plan. Sex and cupidity all mixed up.'

'What about his father?'

'I'm sure that his father didn't know what he was about – any more than his sister did. Rupert, as we know, had been pursuing his own nasty game. But he was a cipher last night. Perhaps the bad news he read in *The Times* really set his teeth on edge. It seems his visit to his dentist was genuine enough.'

'Ambrose?'

'Giles had neglected to do anything about the catch on the front door. So Ambrose walked straight into the house in a tearing rage, and came on his brother as dead as a door-nail. He lost his head, and I'm not surprised. This morning, of course, he realized that Finn was a deadly danger to him. One is rather sorry for Ambrose.'

'I'm not sure that I can find anybody to be sorry for.' Judith paused. 'Except, perhaps, the girl.'

'That's just as well. Bobby will positively require you to be sorry for her.'

'John – no!'

'A passing attraction. I shouldn't worry . . . I'll get that.'

The telephone had rung in another room. Answering it, Appleby was away for some time. When he returned, it was to pour out two glasses of brandy, and hand one of them silently to his wife. He went over to the fire and stirred it – a log fire. Then he turned back into the room.

'That was Tommy Pride,' he said. 'Giles Ashmore shot himself in a London hotel late this afternoon. He's dead.'

MORE ABOUT PENGUINS, PELICANS, PEREGRINES AND PUFFINS

For further information about books available from Penguins please write to Dept EP, Penguin Books Ltd, Harmondsworth, Middlesex UB7 ODA.

In the U.S.A.: For a complete list of books available from Penguins in the United States write to Dept DG, Penguin Books, 299 Murray Hill Parkway, East Rutherford, New Jersey 07073.

In Canada: For a complete list of books available from Penguins in Canada write to Penguin Books Canada Ltd, 2801 John Street, Markham, Ontario L3R 1B4.

In Australia: For a complete list of books available from Penguins in Australia write to the Marketing Department, Penguin Books Australia Ltd, P.O. Box 257, Ringwood, Victoria 3134.

In New Zealand: For a complete list of books available from Penguins in New Zealand write to the Marketing Department, Penguin Books (N.Z.) Ltd, Private Bag, Takapuna, Auckland 9.

In India: For a complete list of books available from Penguins in India write to Penguin Overseas Ltd, 706 Eros Apartments, 56 Nehru Place, New Delhi 110019.

Michael Innes in Penguins

LORD MULLION'S SECRET

Mullion Castle nestles in the heart of rural England, the country seat of Lord Mullion.

Charles Honeybath, RA, has been commissioned by Lord Mullion to paint the portrait of Lady Mullion. With his keen eye for facial features and his unerring nose for human motive, Honeybath perceives a peculiar state of affairs at the stately home.

And with Lady Camilla upstairs, old and infirm of mind, holding the key to the family's past and pecadilloes, the chances of discovering the truth are one in a – Mullion.

THE MICHAEL INNES OMNIBUS

Clues baffle and suspects abound in these exhilarating novels: *Death at the President's Lodging*, *Hamlet, Revenge!* and *The Daffodil Affair*. In them the literary touch of Inspector Appleby is called upon to tackle the macabre murder of a University President, the shooting of the Lord Chancellor while he was acting the part of Polonius, and the simultaneous disappearance of a half-witted girl from London and a half-witted horse from Harrogate.

'A master – he constructs a plot that twists and turns like an electric eel: it gives you shock upon shock and you cannot let go' – *The Times Literary Supplement*

Also published

Appleby and Honeybath
An Awkward Lie
The Gay Phoenix
From London Afar
Seven Suspects

and

The Second Michael Innes Omnibus

PENGUIN OMNIBUSES

☐ *Victorian Villainies*   £4.95

Fraud, murder, political intrigue and horror are the ingredients of these four Victorian thrillers, selected by Hugh Greene and Graham Greene.

☐ *The Balkan Trilogy* **Olivia Manning**   £5.95

This acclaimed trilogy – *The Great Fortune, The Spoilt City* and *Friends and Heroes* – is the portrait of a marriage, and an exciting recreation of civilian life in the Second World War. 'It amuses, it diverts, and it informs' – Frederick Raphael

☐ *The Penguin Collected Stories of*
   Isaac Bashevis Singer   £4.95

Forty-seven marvellous tales of Jewish magic, faith and exile. 'Never was the Nobel Prize more deserved . . . He belongs with the giants' – *Sunday Times*

☐ *The Penguin Essays of George Orwell*   £4.95

Famous pieces on 'The Decline of the English Murder', 'Shooting an Elephant', political issues and P. G. Wodehouse feature in this edition of forty-one essays, criticism and sketches – all classics of English prose.

☐ *Further Chronicles of Fairacre* **'Miss Read'**   £3.95

Full of humour, warmth and charm, these four novels – *Miss Clare Remembers, Over the Gate, The Fairacre Festival* and *Emily Davis* – make up an unforgettable picture of English village life.

☐ *The Penguin Complete Sherlock Holmes*
   Sir Arthur Conan Doyle   £5.95

With the fifty-six classic short stories, plus *A Study in Scarlet, The Sign of Four, The Hound of the Baskervilles* and *The Valley of Fear* this volume contains the remarkable career of Baker Street's most famous resident.

PENGUIN OMNIBUSES

☐ *Life with Jeeves* **P. G. Wodehouse** £3.50

Containing *Right Ho, Jeeves, The Inimitable Jeeves* and *Very Good, Jeeves!* in which Wodehouse lures us, once again, into the ever-green world of Bertie Wooster, his terrifying Aunt Agatha, his man Jeeves and other eggs, good and bad.

☐ *The Penguin Book of Ghost Stories* £4.95

An anthology to set the spine tingling, including stories by Zola, Kleist, Sir Walter Scott, M. R. James, Elizabeth Bowen and A. S. Byatt.

☐ *The Penguin Book of Horror Stories* £4.95

Including stories by Maupassant, Poe, Gautier, Conan Doyle, L. P. Hartley and Ray Bradbury, in a selection of the most horrifying horror from the eighteenth century to the present day.

☐ *The Penguin Complete Novels of Jane Austen* £5.95

Containing the seven great novels: *Sense and Sensibility, Pride and Prejudice, Mansfield Park, Emma, Northanger Abbey, Persuasion* and *Lady Susan*.

☐ *Perfick, Perfick!* **H. E. Bates** £3.95

The adventures of the irrepressible Larkin family, in four novels: *The Darling Buds of May, A Breath of French Air, When the Green Woods Laugh* and *Oh! To Be in England*.

☐ *Famous Trials*
Harry Hodge and James H. Hodge £3.95

From Madeleine Smith to Dr Crippen and Lord Haw-Haw, this volume contains the most sensational murder and treason trials, selected by John Mortimer from the classic Penguin Famous Trials series.

A CHOICE OF PENGUINS

☐ **Small World** David Lodge   £2.50

A jet-propelled academic romance, sequel to *Changing Places*. 'A new comic débâcle on every page' – *The Times*. 'Here is everything one expects from Lodge but three times as entertaining as anything he has written before' – *Sunday Telegraph*

☐ **The Neverending Story** Michael Ende   £3.50

The international bestseller, now a major film: 'A tale of magical adventure, pursuit and delay, danger, suspense, triumph' – *The Times Literary Supplement*

☐ **The Sword of Honour Trilogy** Evelyn Waugh   £3.95

Containing *Men at Arms, Officers and Gentlemen* and *Unconditional Surrender*, the trilogy described by Cyril Connolly as 'unquestionably the finest novels to have come out of the war'.

☐ **The Honorary Consul** Graham Greene   £1.95

In a provincial Argentinian town, a group of revolutionaries kidnap the wrong man . . . 'The tension never relaxes and one reads hungrily from page to page, dreading the moment it will all end' – Auberon Waugh in the *Evening Standard*

☐ **The First Rumpole Omnibus** John Mortimer   £4.95

Containing *Rumpole of the Bailey*, *The Trials of Rumpole* and *Rumpole's Return*. 'A fruity, foxy masterpiece, defender of our wilting faith in mankind' – *Sunday Times*

☐ **Scandal** A. N. Wilson   £2.25

Sexual peccadillos, treason and blackmail are all ingredients on the boil in A. N. Wilson's new, *cordon noir* comedy. 'Drily witty, deliciously nasty' – *Sunday Telegraph*

A CHOICE OF PENGUINS

☐ *Stanley and the Women* **Kingsley Amis** £2.50

'Very good, very powerful . . . beautifully written . . . This is Amis *père* at his best' – Anthony Burgess in the *Observer*. 'Everybody should read it' – *Daily Mail*

☐ *The Mysterious Mr Ripley* **Patricia Highsmith** £4.95

Containing *The Talented Mr Ripley, Ripley Underground* and *Ripley's Game*. 'Patricia Highsmith is the poet of apprehension' – Graham Greene. 'The Ripley books are marvellously, insanely readable' – *The Times*

☐ *Earthly Powers* **Anthony Burgess** £4.95

'Crowded, crammed, bursting with manic erudition, garlicky puns, omnilingual jokes . . . (a novel) which meshes the real and personalized history of the twentieth century' – Martin Amis

☐ *Life & Times of Michael K* **J. M. Coetzee** £2.95

The Booker Prize-winning novel: 'It is hard to convey . . . just what Coetzee's special quality is. His writing gives off whiffs of Conrad, of Nabokov, of Golding, of the Paul Theroux of *The Mosquito Coast*. But he is none of these, he is a harsh, compelling new voice' – Victoria Glendinning

☐ *The Stories of William Trevor* £5.95

'Trevor packs into each separate five or six thousand words more richness, more laughter, more ache, more multifarious human-ness than many good writers manage to get into a whole novel' – *Punch*

☐ *The Book of Laughter and Forgetting*
Milan Kundera £3.95

'A whirling dance of a book . . . a masterpiece full of angels, terror, ostriches and love . . . No question about it. The most important novel published in Britain this year' – Salman Rushdie

A CHOICE OF PENGUINS

☐ **The Philosopher's Pupil** **Iris Murdoch**   £2.95

'We are back, of course, with great delight, in the land of Iris Murdoch, which is like no other but Prospero's . . .' – *Sunday Telegraph*. And, as expected, her latest masterpiece is 'marvellous . . . compulsive reading, hugely funny' – *Spectator*

☐ **A Good Man in Africa** **William Boyd**   £2.50

Boyd's brilliant, award-winning frolic featuring Morgan Leafy, over-weight, oversexed representative of Her Britannic Majesty in tropical Kinjanja. 'Wickedly funny' – *The Times*

These books should be available at all good bookshops or news-agents, but if you live in the UK or the Republic of Ireland and have difficulty in getting to a bookshop, they can be ordered by post. Please indicate the titles required and fill in the form below.

NAME _____ BLOCK CAPITALS

ADDRESS _____

_____

_____

Enclose a cheque or postal order payable to The Penguin Bookshop to cover the total price of books ordered, plus 50p for postage. Readers in the Republic of Ireland should send £1R equivalent to the sterling prices, plus 67p for postage. Send to: The Penguin Bookshop, 54/56 Bridlesmith Gate, Nottingham, NG1 2GP.

You can also order by phoning (0602) 599295, and quoting your Barclaycard or Access number.

Every effort is made to ensure the accuracy of the price and availability of books at the time of going to press, but it is sometimes necessary to increase prices and in these circumstances retail prices may be shown on the covers of books which may differ from the prices shown in this list or elsewhere. This list is not an offer to supply any book.

This order service is only available to residents in the UK and the Republic of Ireland.

● ● ●